Weird of the Skull Totem

Skarde: The Wandering Sword

Erik Waag

This book would not have been possible without invaluable help from:

Daniel P. Riley, Editor. https://www.whimsyland.org/

Dr. John T Parce, Beta Reader. https://johnparce.substack.com/

Krzysztof Porchowski Jr, Cover Art. https://www.artstation.com/krzysztofporchowski

Waag Books

Please visit me at Waagbooks.com or @WaagBooks on Twitter

Copyright © Erik Waag 2024

All rights reserved.

No part of this publication may be reproduced, distributed, or transmitted in any form or by any means, including photocopying, recording, or other electronic or mechanical methods, without the prior written permission of the publisher, except as permitted by U.S. copyright law. For permission requests, contact Erik Waag at erikwaag.books@gmail.com.

The story, all names, characters, and incidents portrayed in this production are fictitious. No identification with actual persons (living or deceased), places, buildings, and products is intended or should be inferred.

Print ISBN 9798876984647

For my Son, Angus.

You are a wellspring of inspiration and support.

Contents

Prologue		1
1.	Chapter One	4
2.	Chapter Two	15
3.	Chapter Three	35
4.	Chapter Four	44
5.	Chapter Five	56
6.	Chapter Six	70
7.	Chapter Seven	86
8.	Chapter Eight	96
9.	Chapter Nine	107
10.	Chapter Ten	119
11.	Chapter Eleven	134
12.	Chapter Twelve	150
13.	Chapter Thirteen	171
14.	Chapter Fourteen	181

15. Chapter Fifteen	188
About the Author	199
Other Works by Erik Waag	200
A Humble Request	201

Prologue

A scream followed by a thunderous crash broke the orderly sounds of the morning work outside.

Three women glanced horrified at each other. Shouts of panic and muffled calls to arms sent shivers of fear down their spines. Each kept a stern expression. Two years spent beyond the borders of safety and civilization tempered even a timid soul, and none of them had ever been timid. From the arrow loops of the room they occupied, they could not have seen what was going on outside. Their imaginations conjured up red-hued fears. Dread had stalked the shadowed corners of their minds for so long, and they wondered only when the black hand of fate would reach out from the benighted lands about them. They, of course, would fight.

A tall blonde woman with resolute blue eyes stood and signaled for the other two to follow her. She sped up the dim stone stairs in powerful catlike leaps three treads at a time to the tower roof. A dark-haired woman reached the crenels first, and her face twisted in cold horror. The tall woman cocked her ear at the terrible commotion before she saw the scene her shorter companion gaped at.

"What is it?" She said as she pulled herself out of the trap door. A sharp edge scraped in her usually steady voice.

The third woman, alluring and dark eyed with sleek black hair, all but flew with practiced ease from the hatch behind her and they met the first, in wide-eyed silence, at the edge of the tower. The tall woman gasped, then quickly regained her composure. She took in the scene before her with a baronial gaze.

The cause of the tremendous crash they had heard moments ago was revealed. The drawbridge gate which secured the front of the castle was down and bridged the stony, steep banked, roaring river that separated the castle gate from the crude road beyond. Dust and debris from its recent fall was still settling about the gaping entrance. Beyond, rolling tendrils of thick morning fog grappled the earth like the arms of some cyclopean sea creature. It could not conceal the hundreds of loping forms racing toward the now vulnerable opening.

Dozens of spear wielding savages had already rushed into the bailey. Their black and white warpaint gave them a grotesque look, and their howls curdled the blood. Soldiers poured out of the inner keep's gate, eager to lend aid to their brothers, almost now overwhelmed by the tide of enemy flooding in.

The two dark haired women looked desperately to the towering blonde for a course of action. Though her face was set with firmness, her eyes quivered with an admix of anger and fear. She gripped the pommel of her sword as if eager to draw it.

"Come!" she shouted, and she flew down the hatch.

Chapter One

"There it is!" Bardano said, pointing at a ship on the horizon.

The merchant vessel had eluded them last night. Though they flew the flag of Zagovar, the easternmost of the Trade League cities, the captain must have been especially skittish as he turned and ran at the sight of them.

"We can close on that in two or three hours," said Ilkar. "Ho! Savo! Do you see it?"

Ilkar, a weather-worn grey-haired pirate, waved wide at Savo, standing in the aft and manning the tiller as always. He waved back and flashed a sign of confidence. Their ship, *The Lion*, turned directly at their prey. Eyeboga called down to the rowers and joined them on the fore castle to gawk at the distant ship. In a flash, the captain leapt up from the lower deck, his long legs taking him two yards for every stride. The giant blonde Northman shielded his eyes from the morning sun and stared off for a long moment.

"Aha!" was all that he said. He grinned at them like a tickled wolf and jumped back to the main deck. "Straight to them, Savo!" he called back to his second in command. "A hearty pace on the oars," he bellowed down the hatch. Savo called out commands and men rushed to adjust the sails.

"Well," Bardano said, "off to the rigging. You two have a turn at the oars, do you not?"

Ilkar grumbled, but Eyeboga gazed out to the seas behind them.

"Do you fear those three Trade-League warships? Surely, they will have given up on us poor pirates after we rounded the Horn and entered the Thardanes sea!"

Eyeboga's dark features pinched in a serious mien. "We did much piracy in their waters. The captains are enraged at the damage we have done. Do not discount them so easily."

"Too much success, you mean!" Bardano said. "Our holds are stuffed with treasure. I hope it does not slow us too much."

"We should all have enough for our whole lives, praise Ozza." Ilkar said, "If only Captain Skarde would show some restraint. He is reckless."

"Do you speak against the giant-slayer?" Bardano said.

"You believe all those stories," Ilkar said. "Giant slayer! You love him so because his tongue is as free as yours, Bardano. Don't give me that look... I do not speak of mutiny. He is a good captain of pirates. Luck is often with him."

Bardano shook his head. "A doubter. Eyeboga, what do you think of Skarde's giant slaying claims?"

Eyeboga looked thoughtful. "He has never made the claim. Others have, and they swear they saw him do it. Still, I have never seen a giant myself..."

"Ho, you three," Tarsazi called as he pulled ropes to tighten the sails. "Less talk. Quick, to your work!"

"Aye! I was just encouraging these lazy louts!" Bardano said. He sped to Tarsazi's aid.

The remaining pair looked at each other exasperated and jogged to the lower decks and the oars. Their eyes took a moment to adjust in the dim, lit only by two open hatches and the slivers of sun that crept between the deck slats. The rower's run smelled of sweat as men grunted and heaved at the oars. The coxswain called out a stiff regular beat, yet not so fast as to exhaust the crew. Two slogging hours past. Ilkar and Eyeboga tensed eagerly as the bustle up top grew. They, and all the men on the oars, heard orders shouted, feet pounding the top deck, and subtle changes in the ship's direction.

"My sword is getting itchy," said Hochnay, a red-haired, wild-eyed man from the North.

Ilkar and Eyeboga laughed together.

"Would you like a moment to yourself?" Ilkar jibed.

"You don't think they'll surrender do you?" Hochnay said. "I hope nae."

"I hope they do," Eyeboga said. "It is less messy."

"I happen to like a good mess," said the red-haired Northerner.

At that very moment Bardano came flying down the hatch, a wild look in his eyes. "Up top and to arms dogs! We are upon them!"

A raucous battle cry went up and thirty of the sixty rowers dashed up the fore hatch, the rest going up the aft. Captain Skarde and his first mate Belgeti stood upon the forecastle, their faces calm, their eyes sharp like hawks contemplating their prey. A dozen of Belgeti's archers knelt low beside them, ready for trouble.

Bardano flew up the rigging on the main mast, cupped one hand to his mouth and bellowed the command of the captain. "Surrender! Surrender to Skarde the giant-killer, scourge of all seas! Surrender and keep your vessel and your lives! Surrender or die!"

Momentum and the winds behind them drove them on toward their quarry. The merchant vessel's gunwale stood higher than their own. Only their captain, his hands raised high in a sign of surrender, and a few others could be seen on deck. A half dozen pirates stood ready to fling grappling hooks, and others readied boarding planks. Just then, the merchant captain let out a cry.

"Crossbows fire!" he yelled, and he jumped down from his high place to hide.

A dozen hidden crossbowmen popped up from behind their gunwale and released a flurry at the forecastle. Skarde, quick as a cat, rolled to the deck. Belgeti and the bowmen dropped low. One man fell back with a gurgle, a bolt sprouting from his throat, and another screamed in agony as a bolt pierced his thigh. The remaining bowmen jumped up and let lose a hail of arrows back at them. So quick they were that the opposing crossbowmen did not all drop low in time, and one of their number fell back dead.

"Have at them!" Skarde bellowed.

He leapt to the deck without touching a stair, and pulled his sword, Morsfangsel, from its fine shagreen scabbard. Hardly had it been drawn before the evil-minded blade whispered into his mind like the low roar of a furnace. *Reach out to me... together we will slay all!* Skarde shook the voice from his head and demanded silence from it.

The grapplers, who had also dropped below the gunwale when the crossbowman let loose, sprang up and threw their hooks. They all caught, and several men heaved on each line. The merchant vessel inched closer. The crossbowmen appeared again, but Belgeti and his archers let them have a volley for their trouble. Two of their own grappling-men fell to the deck in agony, but two of the enemy also fell.

"Faster, dogs!" Skarde yelled. "Quick, throw the gangplanks!"

Before the two vessels abutted the planks were thrown up. Two were tossed aside by the crossbowmen who put aside reloading for the more pressing task of melee. The pirates, however, were eager and swarmed up the planks. One fell screaming to the waves below, and another dodged a sword stroke as he topped the enemy hull.

Skarde bounded forward and was among the first up. He roared and came slashing at the mercenaries who had dropped their crossbows to fight with swords. They parried his blows but retreated foot by foot. Skarde caught one with a mighty swing to the chest. The fools wore chain hauberks – a death sentence if they fell overboard. Though proof against most blades, even steel links could not withstand the unearthly sword driven by Skarde's thickly corded arm. He sliced through links and drew blood, though not a mortal blow.

The mercenary sergeant pressed forward and battered down Skarde's return stroke, saving his man.

"Cease! We surrender!" he bellowed, taking a step back.

Skarde snarled and took a swing at him. He leapt back, a look of horror on his face.

"We surrender! Do you not honor the mercenary's code?" he protested.

"Damn fool!" Skarde bellowed. "Your hopeless fight has cost men their lives!"

"My employer demanded it," the sergeant shot back. "It would be poor form and cowardly to yield so quickly!"

"Keep silent now, and drop your arms," Skarde said. "You might live if your own tongue does not strangle you."

The sergeant smiled and dropped his sword. His men followed his lead. Skarde's pirates flew over the top eager for a fight. The crossbowmen were quickly surrounded and put up no resistance as their hands were tied. Skarde turned as another racket caught his ears. The captain of the ship struggled against two burly pirates as they hauled him closer.

"You'll all hang for this!" he howled. "The Count of Saraylos will not abide pirates in his waters! You fools!"

"Fools?" Skarde spat. "Madman! You fight back against so many with but twenty mercenaries? We offered to you a merciful surrender."

"You do not understand honor, savage. Nor bravery. I hoped a few scratches might send you off. It is my duty as captain to deliver my cargo," he said.

"Honor? T'was they that fought, not you. And what of your crew?" Skarde asked.

"They, too, know their duty and the risks."

Skarde shook his head. "A wealthy fool on an adventure," he said to Tarsazi who stood nearby. "Hold him. Quiet, if mercifully he will cooperate."

"Gather round ye all!" Skarde shouted, waving his sword at those not occupied with the merchant captain and the crossbowman.

Hochnay and Bardano rushed forward, pressed from behind by two dozen others.

"We will rush the hold. Will the fools fight or no? We will give them what they want. Follow me now all!"

A cheer went up. Skarde and his pirates marched to the merchant's forecastle where the crew had disappeared. He battered in the door with a square shoulder. The small forecastle room was emptied, and another door appeared to cover the hatch. Skarde crashed through that in moments.

He barreled downward, roaring eagerly, brandishing his sword, and followed by a pack of his ferocious sea-raiders. In the dim lit hold some fifty men huddled back among the cargo. Some brandished sabers, others daggers, and still more with nothing but battens. Most blanched at the awful sight of pirates.

"You have not the look of warriors. Toss your weapons, and you live," Skarde roared.

The foremost sailor tossed his weapon, and in moments a clatter filled the hold as the rest followed his lead. Several fell to their knees and begged for mercy.

"Hold!" Skarde boomed.

He held back his most eager fighters. *Hochnay*, he thought, *is a savage fighter*. A berserker after his own heart, but dangerous at times like these. He shouted commands and his men settled. They were fuming that the surrender was betrayed, as was he. One by one the trembling crew was taken topside. There they were deprived of pocket and purse, lined up shoulder to shoulder against the length of the starboard rails, and cowed into silence.

The merchant captain brayed. He threatened them for their cowardice and exhorted them, at first, to rise up and fight their attackers, whom they outnumbered. When it was clear that the fight was over, he sited pacts and treaties, and rules of the sea in a plea for his skin.

Skarde's anger rose at the buffoon. He considered clemency, even if his own crew thirsted for blood. Then he chanced to lay eyes on the two dead crossbowman lying on the deck where they had been slain.

"For what," Skarde muttered. He thought of his own casualties. Two at least... He turned his gaze to the captain, and he finally read his fate in Skarde's grim glare.

"Hold me hostage!" The captain pleaded. "I will fetch a princely ransom."

"What of them?" Skarde said, gesturing at the merchant crew.

"What?" Said the captain? "I don't know. There are slave markets west and south..."

"Pah!" Skarde spat. He stormed over to the merchant captain and grabbed him by the scruff. He pressed him forward toward the rails of the ship. The captain struggled, but against Skarde's size and muscle he could not resist without a weapon.

"No!" screamed the captain. "No, you can't! The count will have your head!"

Skarde heaved and tossed the man over the edge. He wailed on the way down, and Skarde turned before he splashed into the black waters. The captain's men stared on with pale, blank expressions. Skarde gestured to his men to continue their work. No need for a grisly delay. The disembarked captain could still be heard splashing and pleading as Skarde approached Belgeti, who stood close to the mercenaries.

"What of the merchant men?" The mercenary sergeant asked business-like.

"What of them?" Skarde said. "They are men not unlike my compatriots. If they do not fight us, we will not harm them."

The sergeant nodded. "And what of us?"

Skarde stared at the man, and though in no position to threaten him he held Skarde's gaze. "Some of my men would see you hang for the needless killing you have caused."

"An argument as fair as any," he said. "Yet killing is my business. Yours as well. Is business not good?"

Skarde nodded. *The cocky bastard is not so unlike myself.*

"To my reckoning, you have killed two of mine, and I have killed two of yours. What need of a further toll?"

"So, you will allow us to leave?" He asked.

"Why not?" Skarde said. "We have what we came for, and these sailors need a new captain... unless you would go fishing for one. That is your business."

The sergeant looked perplexed, as if his good luck was too much to ask for and a surprise was coming. Then he laughed suddenly. "I am Anthrim. Captain Skarde, you say?"

"I do," Skarde said.

"You're a bastard, Captain Skarde, but a fair one! My thanks."

Chapter Two

"Are you sure this is a good idea?" Belgeti said.

Skarde stood upon the deck, lost in his musings. The green coast of Saraylos slipped by. What civilized people lived so far distant in what was called the wild east? What lay beyond the last civilized shores?

"Skarde?" Belgeti called him from his reverie.

"As good or bad an idea as any," he said at last. "We must sail into strange and distant waters for a spell, 'til we shake the warships of the League-Ports from our tail. There will be little chance to go ashore. Already the men have been shipbound for a long while. They are driven to distraction. What use is gold if we may not spend it?"

"Hmm. The young are impatient and in need of amusement. But shall we put into port here? Will not the whole island be aware of our piracy?" Belgeti said.

"*The Lion* is the swiftest ship in these waters. And I doubt that the good sergeant-come-captain would sail straight into the Count's ear? Nay. We will take one day for our leisure. We'll go to a small port on the other side of the isle. No word will have reached them."

Belgeti shrugged. "Don't tie the mooring knots too tightly."

Far ahead down the shore a spire came into view. Skarde's eyes soon made out what appeared to be a beacon, or possibly a watchtower. His right hand instinctively clasped the hilt of his sword. *Who watches us?*

Soon the skyline of a small town rose above the hills and trees of the shore. The bustle on the deck and the stroke of the oars stiffened. Skarde could sense a crackle of excitement in the salt air. *The Lion* swept around a headland and a dozen men gawked as the town crept into view. The men cheered. The low buildings were made of stone and looked well made. Most were short and sturdy, and the town swept back toward a bucolic hinterland. No doubt more than one tavern was concealed within its broad squares.

The men cheered.

Smiling, Skarde caught sight of the long thin stone-work harbor. "Ahoy!" he yelled. "Lower the sails and make port!"

Belgeti appeared at his side, cackling in glee, for the plains-rider was most eager, despite his warnings, to put his feet on land again. "Do you think they have horses?"

"So long as they have ale."

The docks rolled into view and the shapes of the ships moored there revealed themselves. Skarde's brows furrowed, and he felt suddenly ill at ease. Belgeti gasped and grabbed Skarde's arm.

"Look, four ships are moored here... and that one!" Belgeti pointed at a familiar vessel.

"Damn my blind eyes! How did I not see it sooner!" Skarde swore.

Though its sails were furled, Skarde recognized the high castle and elaborate aplustre of the largest of the League-Port war ships. Men swarmed its deck, and even as they drifted by the enemy began unpacking its sails.

"They've seen us." Belgeti said.

"Aye. So much for lightening our pockets," Skarde said, a grim note in his voice. "Hike the sails and row!"

Four dozen men heaved on oars in a slow, stiff rhythm. The deck stank of the sweat that drenched their hair and trickled down their pained backs. Grumbles could be heard here and there, between the creaking wood and the regular splash of oar blade against sea water. None looked back at Skarde with a begrudging eye, for he, too, set his rough palmed hands to an oar. He had rowed with them all day.

They had sailed straight east all night after their close scrape with the mighty warship. As the sun rose, the strongest men took the oars and they put forth all speed. The thought of a fruitless battle with a superior foe put fire into their strokes, and they cut through the waters like a sea bird about to take flight. As the sun sailed high into the sky and the dim rowing deck became warm and sweaty, their enthusiasm waned, and their muscles groaned. Skarde grit his teeth and pulled his oar as hard as any two men, and so none complained about the effort demanded of them.

Skarde glanced back as the hatch above him darkened. There, loomed Belgeti, a dark figure against the bright blue sky.

"What news?" Skarde asked.

"Doesn't your stomach grumble? Night comes. Men want food!" Belgeti said.

"It grumbles as much as anyone's... you are right," Skarde said. He drew a deep breath and set his oar in a brace that held it high out of the water. He stood and stretched, groaning loudly, hoping to release all the day's soreness. "Men!" He called out. "We have labored all day, almost without respite, and you have all done your part and more! I thank you! Your efforts succeed! We are not pursued! Let us rest and eat."

A cheer went up, and voices erupted in conversation with their mates. Skarde turned and strode two paces to the steep stairs at the bottom of the hatch and eyed Belgeti with an optimistic glance.

"We aren't being pursued, are we?" Skarde said softly.

Belgeti shook his head. "No sign of any ships."

Skarde smiled and bounded up the steps as Belgeti made way. He winced at the brightness of the sky, despite the orange and purple tinges on the horizon. He inhaled deep the sea air and smiled at his friend.

"We've done it, I'm sure. Neither the navy of Saraylos nor those three ships of the League-Ports will find us!"

Belgeti shrugged. "If we were being followed by horsemen across the plains, I would say we should stay in the saddle and ride on."

"What about here on the sea?"

He shrugged again. "My horse would sink!"

Skarde smiled. "You'll sink if you don't watch your tongue. Still, we'll keep sailing east, at least over this night. What then? I'm feeling bold again! We must consider our next quarry."

Belgeti nodded. "The coast to the east is a wild land of savage reputation. To the north-east is the Kthonva sea. There are, by the word of some crewmen, a few fortified towns, and some ships sail in trade."

"Perhaps we will try that way. I would not have come this far east only to run with my tail between my legs. We shall have a victory, then head south and west again... in a wide loop," Skarde said.

"And then we might sail northwest and set upon ships there like a storm."

"See, Belgeti... you sound like a born pirate already."

They, and most of the crew, ate their sup standing at their duties or resting for a moment on the rails or ropes. Skarde, Belgeti, Savo, and Farasid gathered in the captain's quarters. Space was set aside for one desk, and the rest was packed with food, loot, and crates and barrels of things that Skarde didn't want in the damp lower deck. They crowded about the small desk as Savo unrolled one of the maps that the Iron Brotherhood had kindly left on board when they stole the ship. Skarde gnawed upon a bone, half stripped of flesh, and glanced at the sketching.

His mind was drawn back to thoughts of Sulmei, even as the men spoke. The cabin had been hers before she left for parts unknown, and now, he used it as a storage room. It was almost a shrine to some of the men, as if she were some patron goddess, and he would not profane its mystique. In any case, he preferred to sleep in common quarters with the crew. He thought of the strange, indecipherable maps in her strange eldritch book. His mind wandered for a moment of her strange tale, and the strange journey she proposed to embark on. And, of course, he thought of her strong supple body, and her unquenchable desires... and suddenly, he sensed an angry shiver in the sword hanging from his belt.

You still desire her blood, O vengeful blade?

"Captain? Are we agreed?" Savo said.

"What?" Skarde said. He chided himself silently for letting his mind wander to women like a heart-struck youth. "Yes... our course is simple. We sail as fast as we might due east o'er night, and in the morning, we sail this way," he traced his finger over the map, "north somewhat, if you believe we may come across some merchant vessel to plunder."

Savo nodded. "I know little of the towns that have sprung up in the wild lands beyond the Savage Mountains, but they are there, and to trade they must come through these straits. I expect they will not be so easy to cow into submission. Men are harder in uncivilized lands."

"No doubt they are. But we will have some plunder before we take an easy-going trip west again. That is our course."

They nodded in high spirits and drank their ale and ate their dinners. Finishing quickly, Skarde roamed the deck to scan the horizon one last time. It was as empty as a desert. He barked orders, he helped to set the sails for the night, and he spoke with the man on till. Only when the deck settled into pitch-quiet did he retrieve his blanket. The waters were cold and brought a chill to the still night air. Still, Skarde preferred to sleep with the stars as his roof. He nestled against the hull at the aft end of the ship, not far from the tiller in case something was spotted on the horizon. There he slept, and there he woke just as the pre-dawn sky was tinged with violet and blue. Skarde greeted the sun with a wolf's smile and strode to the till-man.

"Smell the air!" Skarde said. "It is fresh and swift. I think we will see action today. Turn us half to the north!"

"Aye," he said.

The crew roused from their slumber. A warm wind blew from the south. Skarde and Tarsazi organized the men to work the rigging to take advantage of the shift. They picked up speed after their work was completed, and the men began heading below decks. They needed little prompting to the labor of rowing, though they rubbed their sore muscles from the previous day.

Even as they descended, a fog began to form over the cold waters beneath them.

"I should hope rowing is light today," Skarde overheard a man say.

"Nay," said another. "We should row swiftly and turn straight north. The shores to the east are haunted. This fog comes not by chance... it might conceal ghosts!"

Skarde smiled, though he disapproved of spook-talk among his men. The others about him laughed.

"Not every fog is a cloak for phantoms, Serigios!" said one of the skeptical men.

"Not all fogs, but this one be," Serigios said.

Skarde strode up to the men and looked over the teller of ghost tales. He was short, stoutly built, and strong limbed. His skin was darkly tanned. He had the look of the fisherfolk of the archipelago marking the east end of the Thardanes sea.

"And how do you know those shores are haunted? Have you been there?" Skarde said.

"No, no, Captain," Serigios said. "But I have heard many tales. I was a mason before I was enslaved – when I lived on the isle of Damalos. We move around a lot, we masons, looking for work, you see. Well, we hear tales from men a-close and from men a-far. Sailors used to say – don't you never sail east of Saraylos. Phantoms and the living dead live in the forests of the coasts to the east!"

"But you've never sailed east of Saraylos," Skarde said.

"No, no, Captain, not 'til just now. But that fog gives me a chill. I don't hope to sail too far into it."

"Fair enough," Skarde said. "We aren't looking for a port or a shore, but a ship to loot. Forsooth, no more ghost stories!"

"Aye, aye," he nodded.

Serigios and the others went below deck and rowed, while Skarde kept order up top. He spoke to the lead men, adjusted their course, and watched the fog thicken about them. He gazed into the rolling mists, willing his eyes to pierce their veil, and in the swirls, a ghostly skull the size of a ship appeared. A chill touched pierced him. It dispersed as quickly as it formed, and Skarde laughed at himself.

"What do you see?" asked Belgeti, who stood nearby.

"I see myself becoming a fool who listens too closely to fireside tales."

"You should trust yourself. Even fools are right, sometimes," Belgeti said.

"Ha. What do you think? Is it wise to sail through a haunted mist and seek for more ships to plunder?"

Belgeti shrugged. "I've seen worse mists. Maybe your plan is impetuous, but too much caution might be a worse flaw for a pirate captain."

"Aye, that is my gut feeling. But we sail into waters unknown to most of the men... and myself... and I wonder if they are uneasy. Talk of ghosts!"

"Yet you speak to your sword. Does it not house the dread spirit of a vengeful giant?" Belgeti said.

Skarde raised and eyebrow and stared hard at his friend. "Aye. But I saw the giant with my own eyes."

"And some men have seen ghosts with their eyes."

"Your arrow strikes close enough. So be it. When *I* see ghosts... and not phantasms in the mist... I shall turn the ship about. Until then..."

Belgeti nodded. "Find a fat merchant ship to loot, and all their fears will be forgotten."

Satisfied, Skarde descended to the rowing deck and took up an oar. The mist began to fill the dimly lit space, a silver-grey haze that clung to the wood and deepened the pitch of the creaking oars. Skarde's ears twitched as Serigios' tale was whispered back and forth. The men looked wide eyed at the rumor, but then smiled and shook their head. The sea, just visible outside the ports, had a dream-like, otherworldly quality, and the men's faces seemed to drift in whimsy as they pulled on the oars. The day darkened as the fog thickened. Quite suddenly it lifted, as if they had sailed into a new world. Hardly had the rowing deck lightened when Belgeti leapt down the hatch.

"Captain! A ship!" he said.

Skarde stood, and the rowers ceased their labor to turn their heads.

"Keep rowing, men. We'll want speed one way or the other."

Skarde dashed up the stairs with Belgeti as the men doubled their efforts. Skarde and Belgeti stood beside Savo and Tarsazi, who peered out into the haze. There on the horizon, to the north, stood a pair of bare masts like the black trunks of trees on a hill shrouded by pale autumn fog.

"No sails," Skarde said.

"Aye. They sail against the wind where we sail almost entirely with it," Savo said.

"Hmm. Surely they've seen us," Skarde said.

"Most likely," Savo said. "Hard to say if they are running, giving us wide berth or coming right at us."

"Ah, and look," Belgeti said, gesturing at the open sea to the east.

There, thick tendrils of fog stretched out and engulfed the ship again. They shifted from side to side hoping to catch a glimpse of the mysterious vessel, but it had disappeared. Skarde pondered the sighting.

"Belgeti," said he, at last. "Get your archers together on the chance that we fight. Tarsazi, get Grim-Face and round up the best fighters. We must keep to our posts, but be ready."

Belgeti and Tarsazi nodded and went about their tasks. Skarde ran below decks and announced to the rowers to be at the ready for a fight. He returned to the top and paced the deck, looking again and again in the direction they had last spotted the ship. He gripped the pommel of his sword, Morsfangsel, and it felt hot. *Where is that damnable ship? Why does this fog come now to vex me?*

"Captain!" Belgeti called out. He and his twenty archers stood ready on the deck, and they all glared in the same direction. "There!"

Skarde saw it even as his friend announced the sighting – a dark line revealed wisp by wisp in the fog till the outline of a ship made itself clear. It was much closer now. As it was revealed, it turned head on toward them, and its oars could be seen beating the surface of the pale sea.

"What do you think? A merchant?" Belgeti said.

"Nay, a warship! No merchant would purposefully approach a strange vessel so close," Skarde said.

"But who?" Belgeti asked as he strung his bow, as did his archers.

"It's the fastest of the three League-Port ships, though it flies not its flag. I guess it was sent on ahead to sweep the ocean for our company, and *lo*, they have found us!"

"Shall we run?" Belgeti asked.

"Nay. The wolf has caught *The Lion*! Let's be done with this chase so we might be free to reave," Skarde said before he ran to the mid deck hatch and bellowed orders to the rowers. "We fight, sea dogs! Row lightly and do not tire yourselves. When the order comes, you will all need to row like never before. We will turn a-sudden and ram them."

"Aye, captain, and then a fight?" Bardano called up, leaping from his seat.

"My blood is hot to come to grips with the enemy. Let us attack one alone rather than be attacked by three on terms less favorable," Skarde said.

Bardano laughed and leapt back into his seat to row again. Skarde bounded up the stairs as the galley surged forward. Atop deck, he gauged the distance to the enemy. In just a few moments, there would be blows.

"Turn to port and arc around on their side!" Skarde called out.

"Aye!" Savo called out from the tiller.

"Ready your archers, Belgeti!"

Belgeti grinned and nodded.

"Tarsazi, Farasid, Hochnay! Gather who you can," Skarde shouted. "They may try to board us, and most of our fighters are below deck. They will take a moment to join us. If the enemy visits, we will give them such a welcome!"

Skarde drew his sword and cut the air with two eager swipes. Another ten men flanked him, weapons drawn, and Skarde felt a thrill through his spine. His breath quickened. "Come hither!"

The enemy ship turned in response to their maneuver, and the two ships came at one another. Skarde cursed.

"To port again!" Skarde called.

"We can't turn fast enough, Captain. They would have a good shot at ramming us," Savo warned.

"Then straight on!" Skarde roared.

He ran up the steps of the forecastle, stood above the prow and felt the spray of the breakwater on his face. The enemy ship, now only a few ship lengths away, came barreling at them. That ship was a little larger than *The Lion*, and its own forecastle a little higher. Upon that forecastle stood a man with a short red chiton cinched about the waist with a double wrapped leather belt. A red cap embroidered with gold and with a long black tassel draping down over his shoulder distinguished him as captain. He held in his hand a naked blade, shaped like a long thin leaf, and his eyes were ablaze in menace. Skarde stared back at him defiant, his brows furled.

The bows of the two ships raced at each other. Skarde stood with his feet planted wide. Though the enemy ship was bigger, his ship was well made and sturdy. *Our ram shall score and theirs will not*, Skarde willed. Yet as impact seemed inevitable, the two ships drifted out of line, perhaps by the subtle hands of the tillers.

The ships collided, starboard against starboard. The buffet sent Skarde off his feet, but he hopped forward to stay upright, landing with the reflexes of a cat. As the ships grinded, two dozen crossbowmen hidden by the enemy ship's hull sprang up to fire upon him. Just as he had suspected.

Skarde had stood upright, a clear target right until the impact. He presented a prize target, and he had planned to draw some fire away from Belgeti and his archers. He threw himself to the deck and bolts whizzed over his head. His own archers were quick on the mark. Skarde heard their arrows hissing through the air. Enemy crossbowmen screamed and gurgled their last breath. Skarde raised his head and saw Belgeti and his men low to the deck. They cheered mightily. One archer clutched another who suffered a bolt through his shoulder, but even he wore a battle-grin and was pleased at the exchanged.

Skarde bounded to his feet and leapt off the forecastle without touching stairs. "To arms! Rowers to arms!" he bellowed.

The enemy sent several grappling hooks flying over their rail and the speeding ships lurched to a halt, locked to each other. Belgeti's archers sprang to their feet, arrows nocked and awaiting assault. Skarde heard the cries of war below deck, but already, the enemy sent several boarding planks with steel spikes crashing down on the top deck of *The Lion*. Upon these board bounded enemy soldiers bearing long oval shields. Belgeti's archers unleashed their shafts, but most bounced off the shields. Only one enemy fell to the deadly rain.

With fire in his blood, Skarde roared a battle-cry and sprang into the oncoming men right behind the arrows. Before the enemy had even set foot upon their deck, Skarde swept out with Morsfangsel. The razor-sharp blade crunched into a boarder's leg just under his knee, and he toppled into the sea with a bloody arc following him. Another soldier took his place and swung down at Skarde, who knocked the blow aside hard enough to numb his opponent's hand. Now, two foes were at his side. He leapt back and dodged their vicious swings.

Tarsazi fought nearby, backing up as two enemy stabbed and swung at him. Hochnay's piercing battle wail sent a thrill down Skarde's spine and spurred his attacks. The mad-man's wild fury held back several cautious attackers as they awaited help. And help came for the enemy. Soldiers dashed along the boarding planks or jumped the gap between the hulls. Skarde's own men now came rushing up through the two hatches from below deck, but not fast enough. *They hope to overrun us before we can fight back. Well, they'll get a fight!*

He bellowed again and swung hard to his left. He sprang back lest he be stabbed from his right, but now one of his pirates fought beside him. Inspired by the camaraderie, Skarde swung out and hacked that soldier's neck that had almost stabbed him, and his head dangled to one side, almost separated from his body. He turned to fight the enemy soldier behind him, but now two more had joined him. His pirate companion screamed as a sword stabbed his guts. Skarde hurled himself back but could only do so once or twice more before he would be forced to hop into the sea.

"Hells!" Skarde swore.

You will die, he heard a voice say, deep and haughty. *Give yourself over to me. Let go, and I will share my power with you.*

"What do you want?" Skarde shouted. He cared not if his enemy thought him crazed as he slashed and parried.

In the end – revenge! But for now, give yourself over to me and share my power. We shall slay them all. Kill as one!

His sword felt hot again. Mor's spirit burned eagerly within. Skarde felt disgust. *No!* He would not give himself up, even for a short time, to the spirit of the inhuman giant. Already, he felt as if the monster's fingers were wrapping about his mind.

"No!" he bellowed.

Rage. His rage consumed him, and he fought with unmatchable strength against both the spirit in the sword and his foes before him. His arms swelled as he brought his sword down upon his foe's neck in a reckless attack. The soldier's head went tumbling to the deck, followed by a red fountain. In the very same stroke, his sword bit into another soldier's arm, who reeled back with a scream of pain. He spun and kicked at another who's sword would have hacked his back if he had not moved like a whirlwind. Skarde turned to face that one, and several others, as he recovered.

"I am Skarde!" he yelled. "None shall rule me!"

Eyes wide at the berserk Northman before them, the enemy took a step back. Skarde rushed to assault them, but they gave way, dodging and parrying in desperation. He ran to a knot of his compatriots, who battled the archers and the pirate swordsmen. Two soldiers lay dead nearby, but many more pirates. Hochnay bellowed as several foe surrounded him, a red-haired beast. He held them off with furious strokes of his sword, but he was bleeding from several wounds.

Skarde pressed forward, his teeth clenched in desperation as he hacked with the strength of several men. Though a few enemies still boarded their ship, now the charge of the men from below deck came in earnest. They joined the fray eagerly, knowing that defeat meant death. They fought like every swing was their last. Skarde stabbed an enemy through his guts, and to his left, one of his own pirates screamed in agony as his guts also spilled. Their swords painted the deck of *The Lion* crimson.

"Back! Back, men!" bellowed the enemy captain.

He stood still on his own ship, amid starboard. Skarde glared up at him, despising the man like no other. Was it cowardice or prudence that he did not join his crew in slaughter? And now, as things had not gone as easily as he had hoped, he recalled his men. Skarde despised him with a burning fire. Skarde's thicky corded leg muscles propelled him and he leapt upon a boarding plank in a flash at the scoundrel.

The enemy captain's eyes widened as the blonde bearded giant swooped up at him. "To me, fools! Now!"

The red-capped captain swung his sword hard, and their weapons sparked in a clash. Skarde swung back, and the blow was deflected. They fought for a moment as the captain called for his men. In moments, they came swarming over the rails. In a pique of fury Skarde abandoned all caution, his muscles burning, and he brought his sword down upon his foe with thunderous power. His opponent's leaf shaped sword snapped and Skarde's blade slashed him from his face to his chest. Blood erupted forth as he tumbled back.

"Fire! Give them the fire!" he wailed with his last breath.

Skarde dodged a half dozen attacks. He was surrounded, and he ran, hopped upon the rails, and jumped recklessly over the water back to his ship. Their decks were now clear but some of his own men were scrambling up the boarding planks to assault the enemy on their own ship. Skarde's heart swelled. He yearned to follow them back and fight. Yet his bloody stroke against the captain had sated his bloodlust enough that a prudent thought at least came to his mind. Skarde spotted an enemy officer and sailor hauling the limp body of the enemy captain away from the fight. *Kill them all in a savage melee or save our strength for piracy?* He knew what had to be done even through a red haze.

"Let them flee! Back to the ship, men! Back!" he shouted.

Biting back their lust for battle at their captain's commanding voice, the men halted and grudgingly returned, their eyes still ablaze. Those pirates of more even keel, led by Eyeboga, began hauling up the spiked boarding planks and tossing them into the water. The enemy, too, seemed eager to depart. They chopped the ropes that bound them to the grappling hooks.

No sooner had the last rope been cut when a dozen small earthenware pots topped with flaming rags came flying at their hull. A pirate screamed in agony as one cracked open at his feet and flames engulfed him. Eyeboga threw himself away from one just in time. He swatted the flames on his breeches as two others nearer the aft of the ship wailed, their forms alight. They threw themselves into the sea in hopes of dousing the flames.

"Nine Hells!" Skarde swore. "What deviltry?!"

Across the growing gap between the ships, the enemy officer who had dragged away their captain stood laughing and enjoying the sight of his revenge. A last flaming missile hurled across the gap and struck the side of *The Lion*. Flames licked the outside of the hull, joining with those on the blazing deck.

·

Chapter Three

Men scrambled across the deck. Skarde shouted orders as he dashed to the captain's quarters. They were hardly needed. Inside were stored some of the fine red cloaks of the officers of the Iron Brotherhood. He grabbed several and bolted back out on to the deck. His fellows beat flames off the immolated pirate, now writhing on the deck-boards, their torn shirts useless. Skarde tossed a cloak over him to snuff the flames and patted him down. His hands and thighs burned from the heat, and the man beneath him ceased writhing. He pulled the cloak away. His crewman was still, horrifically burned, and quite dead.

At that moment, a hail of crossbow bolts pelted the deck and six men screamed and fell. Three of those writhed for a moment as their life flickered out. Skarde ran to the starboard taffrail to confront the receding ship's crew. He gestured a curse at the enemy officer.

"You son of P'thon! If ever I get my hands on you, you will beg for death!" Skarde shouted, to his foe's amusement.

The breeze shifted and Skarde was singed by dancing flames. He threw himself back from it. Around him, men tossed buckets of water on the blazes, and others hauled more water from the sea.

"Fight the flames first, then tend to the men!" Skarde shouted. "If our ship burns, we will all die."

He cast about for a bucket, but they were all in use, so he beat at flames with the ruined cloak. The fire was tenacious, and he cursed again and again as the flames sprouted back up where he thought they had been beaten down.

"Captain Skarde!" a pirate yelled, wide eyed. "We are taking on water!"

"Nine Hells!" Skarde said. "Show me!"

The pirate led him down the aft hatch. "I sought whatever I might find down here to douse the flames, and look!"

Skarde followed, and their feet splashed in shallow water. Between the desperate yells and stomping feet above them, a hiss could be heard, and the stink of burning pitch. A bright dollop of flame dribbled in through a blackening hole in the starboard hull. Skarde swore a curse as red as the flames eating his ship, and he flew back up.

"Pour your buckets out here! Our hull is blazing above the water line!"

He rounded up a dozen pirates and ordered them to douse the baleful flame. Skarde swore as the damnable inferno burned still after they were soaked, and a second or third bucket was needed to extinguish them finally. After much effort, the flames were out. The pirates looked with clenched jaws at their deck. What was not painted with blood was charred wood. Leaning over the taffrail, Skarde examined the hull. Belgeti came also to look at the damage.

"A gift from Luwydi," Skarde said.

"A gift?" Belgeti said. "A strange thing to thank a god for."

"Luwydi's gifts are rarely reason for thanks. He is a trickster."

"What now?"

"I can see water leaking in. We are sinking. Men!" Skarde called out. "Ye all with buckets... you hauled water in, now haul it out before this ship becomes our tomb!"

Pirates rushed down the hatches. Skarde called for Serigios, Eyeboga, and two others. He motioned for them to follow him down the hatch to the rowing deck. Their eyes widened as they stepped into the flooded hull, already up to their knees. Two dozen men scooped buckets of water and tossed them out the rowing ports. They approached the crumbling, blackened hole in the hull.

"You were carpenters and masons in your life before slavery and piracy. Can you fix this?" Skarde said.

Eyeboga knelt down and eyed the damage with knotted brows. He reached out and tugged on a charred splinter. It snapped off and sea water poured in all the quicker. "Ay-ah! This is not good!" he said.

The others examined the damage. They pursed their lips and shook their heads. Eyeboga looked back at Skarde, his eyes firm and serious.

"I was a carpenter, never a ship builder. Yet who could fix this without a dry-port to work?"

"No, no," Serigios said, rubbing his forearms absentmindedly. "I might be able to hammer nails straight, and I have worked with wood at times... perhaps we could stem the flow."

The four looked back and forth at each other, but none came forward with a clear plan.

"Do what you must," Skarde said. "Tear up the top deck for timbers, and work as you see fit. We must bail the ship as you work, and the less water coming in, the better. Curse this eastward flight! I should have fought them when first they threatened us!"

Skarde strode to the stair of the aft hatch, kicking a spray of water before him, and went up. Some of the men were now attending to the wounded and dead. As captain, Skarde felt he should take the lead in those grim matters out of respect, as well as due to his station. *No time*, he lamented. He signalled to Belgeti, Grim-Face, Farasid, Savo, and Tarsazi, and marched to the captain's quarters. He pulled the maps out again as the other men came in and tossed them on the table. One, with the words 'The map of Sultan Yadak' written across the top had a few scant details of the far eastern coast.

"We are sinking," he said. "I have put skilled men to the task of repairs, but the hull is burnt and crumbling. I know not how far we might sail before the end."

Grim-Face smoothed out the map and jabbed his finger on a group of small islands. "Here, we might land if we turn and sail west right away. It will bring us close to Saraylos."

Skarde pulled his beard. "These are closer than the eastern coast, but too close to Saraylos. Are they under Saraylosian rule? What is this country on the mainland to the north? Zovas?"

Savo stepped forward and swept his hand across the map. "All lands east of the Savage Mountains are wild, and those lands just west are nearly as untamed. Zovas is more a name for a collection of tribes than a proper nation. As for the islands, they are independent, but under Saraylosian thumb."

"I sliced that captain nigh in twain, but his lieutenant lives. They will sail back and report the battle. No doubt there will be eyes out for us," Skarde said. "What of the shores to the east?"

"Haunted, the men say," Farasid said.

Skarde chuckled. His doubt about these rumors was waning. "Perhaps. But I would rather chance a rumor of a phantom than a known and ready threat."

"It may or may not be haunted, as you say, but it is entirely savage. Stories abound," Savo said. "In either chance, there are no ports."

"That is a matter of concern. With no port, repairs will be difficult," Skarde said.

"We could beach the ship at high tide," Savo said. "Repairs would be makeshift, but they could be done."

"If we are discovered by an enemy ship, or attacked by some native tribe, we would be in a bad position," Tarsazi said.

"What if? What if?" Skarde said. "Your caution is warranted, but I have decided. We sail east. I am no soothsayer but I like our chances better in wild lands. Some trouble will befall us, but that is not a present fact. Often the unexpected has legs, while the expected sleeps. Only the Gods may glimpse what is ordained. Even still, men may keep a hand on the rudder of fate, no matter which way the winds of the world blow. Whatever befalls us, we shall fight."

They sailed on for a miserable day, and the men grumbled. Skarde set as many as he could to rowing. The water rose past their ankles and soaked them through. An equal number set to the never-ending task of bailing water. Despite their efforts, the water rose inexorably, even as Eyeboga directed a few men in repairs, and Serigios tore up the top deck. Men paled and looked at each other with haunted eyes as the ship began to slow, so heavy laden with water it was. At last, the carpenters had some success, and the leak slowed, though the breach was not wholly sealed.

At night, they fared little better. Skarde himself worked the oars with many who forwent sleep. Those that did sleep, older men for the most part, did so atop deck for no rest or dry bed was to be found below. The men ceaselessly bailed the water, and fatigue set its grip upon all. A sea mist rolled in, and the men quieted. When Skarde did catch a snippet of conversation, he heard talk about ghosts. Frustrated at the spook-talk, Skarde climbed the rigging ten feet up and addressed the crew.

"Never mind the ghosts in the fog! They do us all a favor and hide us from enemy ships!"

He jumped down, and the men averted their eyes from his gaze. Skarde was not so glad of the fog himself. It might have shielded them from enemy eyes, but he doubted there would be any. They weren't clear on their direction, and they would have trouble spotting land. Even the wind began to die down, and he cursed all the gods he could think of save Ruen. He was not as superstitious as most, but cursing the mercurial Lady of the Sea while in her domain seemed foolhardy.

The Sun glowed pale through a diaphanous haze all afternoon. As it sank his eyes sought to catch sight of land. Skarde stood at the bow of the ship atop the forecastle. Sailing through the night could very well mean sinking beneath the waves. Skarde's lips pressed together, and his grim eyes narrowed. As he was tempted to fall into a melancholy mood, some hint of a form appeared in the mist.

"Savo! Savo, come forth!" Skarde called across the deck.

Most of the crew on deck turned their eyes toward him, and Savo, leaving the tiller to another man, jogged across the deck. He joined Skarde, and the two stared across the misty sea for a long while. All trace of the shape Skarde had seen disappeared.

A few other men gathered about them and joined in the silent watch. Suddenly, the mists thinned, and a shore revealed itself, perhaps an hour's sail in the distance.

Skarde smiled, and the men let out a raucous cheer. The mist continued to disperse, and Skarde discerned a grey-green shore of trees. Beyond that, a mountain appeared that looked as if it had been struck with a gigantic axe. It was as two peaks coming together, split by a deep cleft.

"No! We cannot land here!" Serigios bellowed.

Skarde turned on him, a flash of anger in his eyes, hoping to silence any tall tales. But Serigios eyes were wide as if the pits of hell had been opened.

"That is, it! The Land of the Lamae! Monsters! And there is the mountain cut in two, just as the tales tell! The mountain itself split and the demons of the underworld come forth! We can not land here!"

"Silence fool!" Skarde spat. "We'll sink in hours. What does it matter it the fish eat us, or demons?"

"We can not land there! We will die. They will eat us!" Serigios raved.

"Silence, you will set off a panic!" Skarde bellowed.

By dint of exhaustion and by the power these tales had over him, Serigios raved. The men stared on, mouths agape. Like a striking snake, Skarde punched him in the chin. Serigios stumbled back in a daze and fell to the deck.

"Nine Hells!" Skarde said. "Belgeti, you have some skill as a healer. I do not mean to harm him, but his ravings will lead us to a riot. See that he is well… and if he wakes, give him a mouthful of strong wine."

Belgeti nodded. "I don't think he is dead. He'll be fine. Eyeboga, help me carry him to the captain's quarters."

As Belgeti and Eyeboga carried him down, Skarde turned to Savo. "The tide?"

Savo held his head high and sniffed the air, as if his nose would inform him. "I reckon high tide will come soon."

"Well, at least that bit of luck has come our way. Let's make the most of it. You set our rudder straight for that shore, and I'll row with the men and double their efforts!"

"And if there are rocks?" Savo asked.

"We swim," said Skarde.

Chapter Four

Savo, with impressive nautical skills, had beached *The Lion* safely. Skarde watched the ship list on to its unburnt port hull as the tide went out. He was mesmerized by the slow swaying ship as the water lowered minute by minute until it rolled gracefully on its side. Water poured out of its oar ports to drench the beach, and finally, it was at rest.

"Now, the damage is clear," Savo said as he looked at Eyeboga, shaking his head. "I wonder how we made it ashore!"

"We still can take finished boards from the decks," Eyeboga said, "and start to cover the damage. I hope we have enough tar on board for the patch. We will need a few trees for extra wood."

Serigios rubbed his chin and eyed the treeline as much as the burnt hull. "I will stay here and scrape the hull."

Skarde laughed. "I think that best, man." He turned to the others and bellowed orders. "It is late. Gather wood for fires tonight, you men! You others, take supplies of tools, food, and ale from the ship. We will rest tonight and at sunrise, we will begin repairs in earnest. Let's go!"

The men murmured among themselves and went about their appointed tasks. Belgeti approached him. "I will gather wood, too... my legs want for solid ground," he said.

Skarde smiled. "Solid and dry. Let's go."

They walked the coarse pebble strewn beach, and Belgeti looked back at the beached ship when they were well out of earshot of the men. "If the League-Port ships or one of Saraylos' find us like this they could easily destroy our ship, and claim advantage over us."

"Aye," Skarde said. "We should not linger here long."

"Lighting fires... is that wise?" Belgeti asked.

"No doubt, it isn't. But the men are tired and spooked by ghost tales. Let them have one restful night. We will need more caution the longer we stay."

Belgeti grunted. "It's too bad we don't have fresh meat."

"And wine, and women," Skarde added and Belgeti chuckled.

There, at the edge of a grove of beech and poplar, they collected fallen branches. Skarde felt the warmth of the dipping Sun on his back and smelled the air of late day. They had little time left to gather. Though grey clouds rolled overhead, the long red rays of the dying sun dove deep into the forest. They illuminated a strange image that made the hair on Skarde's neck rise. A supernatural fear sent a chill down his spine as no threat of man ever could. He froze and fixed his eyes, wondering if his imagination and the hysterical fears of Serigios had affected him. Belgeti noticed his companion's bearing, and also looked.

"What is it?" Belgeti whispered, just loud enough for Skarde to hear.

"Look," Skarde said, pointing. I thought I saw one of Serigios' spectres, then just a man... but it moves not."

Skarde bent and put his collection of sticks to the ground, then padded forward, his eyes darting this way and that. He pulled his sword from its sheath. Belgeti followed likewise and gripped his bow. A few dozen paces in, Belgeti saw what had caught Skarde's eye, and he gasped. Skarde approached the apparition of fear. Three human skulls were bound to a tree with long twisted vines and twigs. The primitive ropes and the limbs of the tree created the illusion, from afar, of some undead horror of death and gangling limbs.

"Tomog's children," Belgeti swore. "What an evil sight!"

"A warning?" Skarde said. His eyes darted between the darkening trees.

"I'd take warning, whatever the maker of this thing meant," Belgeti said.

Belgeti poked the skulls with the end of his bow and cleared his throat in disgust. They returned to the pile of sticks they had dropped.

"Maybe Serigios wasn't so foolish after all," Belgeti said. "Perhaps we should not light fires tonight."

"Too late," Skarde said as they gathered up the wood. "Look."

Back near the ship, they could see men gathered and wisps of thin smoke rising from among them.

Belgeti shook his head. "Let's keep our eyes open."

"Always," Skarde said. "And Belgeti, my friend... let's say nothing of this to the men."

Night lingered long and heavy clouds lay over them like a shroud. Skarde slept lightly, his ears catching every clank, cough, and nightly forest sound. Even as the pale grey sky of dawn lightened, Skarde roused the men and organised three groups to head into the forest and bring them back fresh timbers. Others, he organized to tear up parts of the deck and begin repairs. Without orders men took it upon themselves to devise a breakfast, and so they ate as the tide came in and out again. As the waters lowered and the ship steadied, those with a hand for craft helped Eyeboga mend the hull.

Eyeboga wiped the sweat from his brow. The Sun peeked in and out of the clouds, but despite the partial shade, it was a humid day for shipbuilding. He pressed at a board ripped from the hull, his muscles straining to bend it, and knocked nails in as another crewman braced it with his foot. As they struggled to get the hull planks in place, a group of men returned, dragging with them roughly cut timbers. Eyeboga stood and watched them.

"You are late!" Eyeboga shouted down at one.

"Certainly not," Bardano said. "A job well done can not be rushed!"

"The first team was back an hour ago. Put your timbers with theirs," he pointed.

"Oh, you are the captain, now?" Bardano said.

"Higher up the chain than you." Eyeboga smiled. "Where is Ilkar and his group? They went your way."

"I haven't seen them. They went further on than us. He said the patch of trees we found were too weedy."

Eyeboga shielded his eyes and scanned the treeline. All seemed quiet. He shook his head, impatient to see the old man return. Returning to his work, he and his crew hammered in another plank. Glancing back over his shoulder at the forest from time to time, a worry knotted his stomach as no sign presented itself. At last, he lay down his tools and shimmied down the hull with the rope they had tied to the rails. Captain Skarde, nearby, built a blinded firepit with Serigios.

"Ho, Captain," Eyeboga said, with a polite dip of his head in the fashion of his homeland.

"Eyeboga, man! How go repairs?" Skarde said.

"Well enough for a job I have never done before, *ingosi*."

"I expected no magic... that was some terrible damage. Still, we should be off as soon as we might."

"Of course, *ingosi*. I have my concerns about Ilkar and his men, though. They have been gone long."

"Oh?" Skarde said.

"They were to bring back a trunk or two, and not an old giant. They should have completed their labours long ago."

Skarde's eyebrows furled. "Who saw them last?"

"Bardano," Eyeboga said.

Five men strode along the pebbled shore with wary eyes. Skarde, taking no chances, led the small band in search of their missing comrades. After sighting the ominous skull totem, he dared not hope their stay would be trouble free. Along with him, he took Bardano, Belgeti, and two of his best archers, Ramzi and Oğuz. The young Bardano all but demanded to accompany Skarde.

"Here is where my men entered the forest," Bardano said. "Fine enough trees this way, and not so far from the ship."

Skarde smiled at *'his men.'*

Bardano continued. "Ilkar and the others went down this way. I don't know how far. Surely not past that rocky spit yonder."

"Seems like a good guess," Skarde said. "Let us explore the paths between where you lost sight and the spit. Don't call out for them. We don't know who is listening."

They prowled now as the shade of the canopy fell upon them. Skarde and Bardano spread apart, looking for any sign their compatriots might have made, or anything out of place. The archers kept their eyes up for any sign of movement between the innumerable tree trunks.

Presently, one of the searchers hissed for attention. Neither Bardano nor Skarde had found a sign, but Oğuz waved them over. He pointed at a tree as they approached. Even from a distance, Skarde could see that it had been hacked, almost halfway through, by an axe. They all gathered close.

"Here, they were," Bardano said. "But why leave a tree cut but unfelled?"

"Where are they?" Belgeti said, looking about as if his eyes could pierce the tangle of trees.

"Good questions," Skarde said. "But at least we know one thing. And that thing gives me heart. There is no axe or rope dropped nearby. They still have those, and their weapons. At least, they did when they left here."

"Let's find them," Belgeti said.

They spread out, and in moments, Skarde caught sight of an unnaturally long and straight stick. Picking it up, he saw it had a sharp flint head upon it.

"Look," Skarde said, examining the weapon. "A javelin! We are not alone, and the locals might not be so friendly. Beware."

They all gazed into the forest with hard eyes. Skarde examined the ground for a good ten paces around the spot where he found the javelin. He found no blood, to his relief, but he found boot prints in the soft earth near a trickling stream. *The damp that hangs in the air and sent mists out to sea to bedevil now aids us,* he thought. The trail was not hard to follow, and Skarde led them on, wary and silent.

The little stream fell down from a slope strewn with mossy boulders and trees, then led them up a low hilltop. There, a ravine formed, and other little streams flowed. The cleft mountain here could be seen rising from beyond a steep and craggy escarpment, blue grey in the distance. Ramzi stood forward and pointed at the sky just above the treeline to the right of the cut in the mountain. The group gazed off, and Skarde noted a thin, hazy column.

"Is that mist or smoke?" Belgeti asked.

"I'd wager it's smoke," Ramzi said. "One or two rises away."

"The trail leads that way, also. Come," Skarde said.

They marched on, wary for any signs. The air seemed heavy, and they felt as if eyes watched them from the trees. As they mounted the next hill, they saw clearly where the column of smoke rose from, just past the next rise. They crept on, gripping their weapons. Skarde could smell the smoke now, and something else. His nose wrinkled at a coppery stench. The acrid fatty odor seemed to cling to his tongue, and a vague feeling of horror crept up his spine. Skarde paused for a moment to take stock of his companions before he rounded a forested hillock from whence the smoke and stink came. Glancing back, he saw his companions hunched over, their eyes beady and troubled.

Something was terribly amiss, but he knew not what. He took one cautious step after another. His breath came heavy. The trees parted and the sickly smoke wafted into view. At the base of the hillock, twenty men camped about the fire with a spit of meat over it.

"P'thon!" Skarde swore. Icy tendrils crept over his skin and froze him in place. He looked out, wide eyed, over a scene of horror.

At the far end of the camp, two of their missing comrades were unmoving and bound to long poles such that two men might carry them. The third, Ilkar, hung upside down from his foot by a rope under a heavy tree branch. His face was ashen, his body drenched in blood. He was missing one leg from the knee down, and one forearm. The white woad and black ash painted men about the fire roasted what appeared to be a human leg. Ilkar's leg. Strips had been torn off of it, and several of the savages chewed on strips of meat that hung from their mouths.

Bardano wailed like a madman and charged toward the primitives in the camp. Belgeti sped forward, arrow already nocked, and let loose a shot.

Unwilling to be the last to act, Skarde wrenched his mind away from the grip of terror and charged, trying to comprehend what he was seeing.

Skarde's sword burned as he dashed toward the cannibals. Arrows sped through the air, one sharp hiss, followed by two more. Bardano's battle cry spooked their enemy even as two clutched their chests and toppled with shafts planted deep. One savage hurled a javelin at Bardano, and it struck his shoulder. He batted the blooded thing away from his body, his charge on undeterred. He stabbed at one of the warriors, who grimaced as he was run through, and Skarde saw his teeth were filed into triangular fangs.

Skarde reached the camp. Two warriors sprang up to challenge him, and one swung an antler warclub. He knocked it aside and countered with a ferocious sweep that separated the man's head from his body in one stroke. He kicked at the other warrior and knocked him back. As he battled the second tribal warrior, more arrows sliced through the air. Two more enemy fell to Belgeti's archers, and Skarde screamed fury as he charged the small gang that had retreated from the cooking fire.

They scattered into the dark woods about them, fleeing before the pirate's sudden onslaught. *Chase them! Kill them!* He felt his sword, Morsfangsel, urge him on more with feelings than words. *No*, he thought. There might be others, and they were outnumbered. Once they discovered that only five pirates had chased them off, they would return with vengeance.

Bardano, however, wailed in wrath and sped off after them.

"Bardano!" Skarde bellowed.

He flew after the younger man. His long legs carrying him like the wind, though Bardano was driven like a bat out of hell. Too far into the forest they had gone, when Skarde dropped his sword and catapulted himself at Bardano to grapple him. They fell to the pebble strewn ground. Bardano struggled and cursed. He punched Skarde, and Skarde returned the blow. Bardano battled on, though the giant Northerner's fist might fell an ox. Finally, Skarde restrained his battle-mad compatriot long enough to look him in the eye.

"Halt, Bardano!"

He glared at Skarde for a moment with wild hate in his eyes. Then a glimmer of thought twinkled in them, though his countenance did not soften. His struggling ceased.

"We must free Ilkar and the others," Skarde said. "Take them back to camp... prepare a defence..."

Bardano came to his senses as Skarde called Ilkar's name. "Aye, captain," he said.

Skarde let him go and rose. He ran back through the forest from whence they had come, and Bardano followed closely.

"I should chastise you for attacking without orders," Skarde said.

"Captain, my apologies," Bardano said, "but those beasts... inhuman!"

"Aye... I would, but I can't. Your impulse was true." Skarde stopped and turned to Bardano. "And their deed inhuman. Ilkar is your friend, aye?"

"He is, the old fool," Bardano said.

"Come, lets hurry."

They continued back to the scene of horror. The archers had cut Ilkar down and lay him on the ground and were examining the other two tied to poles. Skarde jogged to Belgeti's side.

"These two are alive, though they are bloodied and battered," Belgeti said.

Skarde examined their bonds. "Leave them tied. They will not be able to walk back to the ship. We will use the poles to carry them. It seems cruel to me, but we have need of utmost speed. Belgeti and Bardano, carry one, and Ramzi and Oğuz will carry the other.

"What of Ilkar? Does he live?"

Belgeti pursed his lips and looked at Bardano with sad eyes.

Tears whelmed in Bardano's eyes, but he stayed any outbursts. "We can't just leave him here," he said, at last, in a cracked voice.

"No, we will not leave him here to be further mauled by these wicked brutes," Skarde said. "I will carry him on my back."

Chapter Five

Skarde stood staring at the two injured men, still unconscious, as Belgeti and another tended them. His ears, however, were on the crew which crowded about them. Whispers flew around him like a breeze through the autumn forest. Blood soaked his flanks and legs. Ilkar's blood, whose body lay now like cast off refuse on the beach. Some men had already come to conclusions about what had happened, and Belgeti's archers had no doubt murmured about the evil they had witnessed. *I will need to keep order and soon.* He marched to the ship and clamoured up the side of the hull without the use of the rope. From his high vantage, he could see the faces of all the men turned up toward him.

"Gather round all! Gather round and I will tell of our plight without varnish!"

The men left the injured their space and came to a semi-circle just beyond the bowsprit of the ship.

"Tomorrow, we will double our efforts to fix the hull and be off as soon as we might. As you all have now guessed, these shores are dangerous. Some belligerent clan lives in these woods and has set upon three of our men."

Wide eyed, the men gasped and muttered. "Why has Ilkar been dismembered?" cried a voice.

"Is it true," called another, "that these savages ate his flesh?"

Skarde raised his palm to silence the noise and speak, but a shriek broke his concentration.

"It's as I said!" Serigios wailed. He looked wild eyed at the treeline in the growing twilight. "This land is cursed. Madmen and cannibals? There is an evil here driving them!"

"Silence, Serigios! Eyeboga, Farasid, Tarsazi! Take him into the ship and quiet him!"

Skarde watched in dismay as Serigios flailed and screamed as the three men wrestled with him, dragging him around the ship. Restraining his desire to leap to the beach and deal with Serigios himself, he turned his attention back to his men before a riot erupted. He shouted commands and demanded silence, and the crew looked at him, some wide eyes and with a sickly pallor, others with a grim determination and clenched jaws.

"These are a primitive people," Skarde said. "They use stone tools. I, along with Belgeti, Bardano, Ramzi, and Oğuz chased off a score of them... a whole clan's worth of their warriors. Aye, they'll be back, but a score is all they'll be able to muster, or thereabouts, if I guess rightly. They will need to gather others of their tribe from further afield. I wager that we will have two days, or so, before they dare to attack us."

"But we are easy targets on this beach… they will slaughter us out here," bellowed a man.

"I saw no bows among them, only javelins. If they do employ missile weapons, we might take refuge in the boat. We have our own bowmen, and we might force them into close combat in the hum if they are so ardent to slay us."

The crew murmured and argued among themselves, but their panic was held back for the moment. Even those with previously peaceful professions were now used to fighting, and the semblance of a plan calmed their nerves.

"Now, I will take Ilkar. We can't bury him in the forest, and I won't have his body wash ashore. Whoever will shall come with me, and we will build a pyre with whatever kindling we have."

"Won't that draw the cannibals?" Eyeboga asked.

"There is no chance of keeping unseen now, and the light and heat is a comfort. We will leave the fires burning all night," Skarde said. "Tomorrow, we will make the ship sea-worthy, even if slipshod. We may then find a calmer harbor for more adequate repairs."

Skarde surveyed the arc of men about him, measuring the vigour of the company. They were anxious for useful tasks but no longer on the edge of panic. Then an odd sight caught his eyes.

In the twilight gloom under the eaves there stood a man-like shape. A black-hooded menace wrapped in a tattered black cape. It stared back as Skarde as he stared at it, black sockets in a skull visage. His limbs transfixed by fear – a deep soul-striking horror as he looked at what surely was an apparition send from the bleakest netherworld. Then it seemed to melt into the deepening shadows. Skarde drew a breath to call attention to the deathly vision but thought better of it. *What can we do? Chase a phantom through the forest at night and re-kindle the madness consuming the crew?*

Stern-faced, Skarde descended to the beach. The men prepared for the fearful night and continued to murmur among themselves. Right away, Bardano and Eyeboga volunteered to build Ilkar's pyre, and two others wished to go also. They hauled most of their gathered firewood a half mile northward along the beach. Too long, in his mind, did they labor in its building. Darkness descended and Skarde scanned the all-too close vastness of the trees.

"It is good we do this," Eyeboga said. "The men will be heartened to see that you keep to tradition in the face of danger."

"Tradition, Eyeboga, oft guides us to necessities. But tradition or no, I won't give those dogs a chance in Hell at eating any more of our own."

"Captain, you saw something in the trees while you were up on the hull. What was it?"

Skarde raised his eyebrows. He wished Eyeboga didn't catch quite so much, though no doubt it would prove useful. "Just a figment of my imagination. Shadows."

Eyeboga nodded.

Soon, the pyre was built, and the fire set to it. Few words were said among them, and Skarde said none. Skarde noted that Eyeboga shed tears for their elder compatriot as the flames covered his flesh. A grimness dragged down Bardano's young face as he had not seen before. They stood, regarding the flames for a moment, their eyes blinded to the dark forest nearby.

"Come," Skarde said. He saw nothing between the black trunks but felt a chill down his spine at some lurking malevolence.

They returned to camp. Skarde slept as well as any of them, but his ear caught every hoot, chitter, and scuffle from under the nearby eaves. There was no need to post guards. Men rose to scan the treeline often, and some did not sleep at all. No attack came. Skarde rose just as the red glow of morning silhouetted the forest canopy, and the men rose with him. The fires were fed the last of the kindling and work began in earnest.

"There are eyes in the forest," Belgeti said, coming to Skarde as he chewed a slice of dried meat for breakfast.

"Aye," Skarde said. "I can feel them like whispers of an ill wind on my back."

"Shall I gather the archers and a few others and drive them off?" Belgeti asked, wondering aloud.

"Nay. They know we are here, and we know they are there. I doubt you would catch any. They know their home better than we."

"I don't like it," Belgeti grumbled.

"Look. The tide comes in again. I would like a look farther off... and higher up," Skarde said.

He climbed atop the hull and waited until the tide righted the ship, lifting the mast upright. Presently, he crawled up the slanted rigging like a spider. Securing himself in the crow's nest, he gazed out over the forest. Right away, an oddity drew his eye.

"A castle!" he whispered to himself.

He blinked, as if his eyes had lied. "Aye, it is a castle," he spoke to himself as if he needed to be told. "Not a large one, and newly built methinks."

The castle appeared to be founded on a cliff side just under the two peaks of the mountain. Blue grey, it appeared in the hazy distance, and it was too far to make out any inhabitants that might have been on its walls. An escarpment barred passage to the east, save for what appeared to be a slope to the castle's north. He sat and scanned the horizon, while a plan ruminated in his mind.

At last, he descended to the beach before the tide receded. There, he helped the builders chop timbers into useful planks. As the ship rolled back on to its side, men helped to lift planks to the damaged hull. Savo, Eyeboga, and a few others labored in earnest. Belgeti, who had been standing in a line with his archers a few dozen paces further up on the beach, approached him.

"What did you see up there?" he asked Skarde.

"Ha! Now that the heavy lifting is done, you've come by for a chat?" Skarde said.

Belgeti shot him a hurt look. "I couldn't build a wood horse, so what good can I do here?"

Skarde laughed and then stared pensively into the trees. "This is a strange land. The mists bring dreadful visions, drive my men mad, and bring us to a shore with cannibals. I saw a strange thing."

"Stranger than the skulls? Don't keep me on my toes."

"First, I will tell you that earlier, as I rallied the men, I saw a black-cloaked deathly figure in the trees. I said nothing."

"Might it be one of our hungry friends?" Belgeti asked.

Skarde pulled on his beard. "It could be, but some instinct in me says it is not."

"And what is after this first mystery?"

"There is a castle in the distance," Skarde said.

"Hmm," Belgeti said. "I didn't think there was any civilization out here. Are there even farming villages nearby?"

"None that I know of," Skarde said. "I didn't see any break in the canopy that would suggest a clearing."

"Does it guard that cleft in the mountain?" Belgeti said.

"Mayhap. It appears to sit right before the mountain, high up. That escarpment looks to be a cliff high and sheer. I think I could climb it, but many others would not. Perhaps the fortification oversees a pass?"

"We have not the men or tackle to take a castle," Belgeti said. "If there be any garrison, we could only defeat a small force... and only if we get in. Do you intend to take it by subterfuge?"

"I do not intend anything of the sort... not yet. It would be a desperate run to the castle if all goes ill here. Yet, these cannibal savages did not build that stonework. If need presses, perhaps we will discover who did... and if they would like help fighting."

"I'd prefer taking my chances with the sea," Belgeti said, his eyes grim.

"I as well."

Repairs did not go as Skarde had hoped. Eyeboga toiled with the wood he was given, but he was no shipbuilder. The curve of the hull frustrated him, though he showed it not. That is until Savo, intent upon speed, almost came to blows with Serigios, who laboured to heat the pitch in an oven constructed of beach stones. He accused Eyeboga of using too much – more than he could heat on the small structure they had made. Did he intend to make him look bad?

Eyeboga, patient no more, cursed them for trying to direct him in work he knew better of. Skarde broke up the dispute before blows were exchanged, but it was clear they would spend another night on the shores of this eerie land.

As the day waned, the air grew still and warm. The forest seemed quiet and tense. Skarde heard no sound from its eaves.

"Gather what arms you might need and warn the men," Skarde spoke to his lieutenants.

"But why, Captain?" Grim-Face said. "Not a peep from the forest."

"That's what bothers me. Hardly a scratch or a bird call. Something sends a chill down my spine despite the warmth."

"The calm before the storm," Belgeti said to himself. He strung his bow.

"Aye, Belgeti. They are out there. How many, I know not. I feel they will attack, and soon. Sunset approaches and I fear they will try to break us and pursue us in the dark. Get ready. I will set more ropes up over the hull. If we need to move back, climb into the ship. High tide comes soon and will make a good castle of our own for a short while."

They set off to prepare a defense, and Skarde tied a dozen more ropes off the side. The savages could no doubt climb them as well, but once in the ship, defense would be easier. He rushed as some instinct, born of his uncivilized nature, knotted his stomach. He had just finished his job when figures emerge from the bush. A silent wave of savages coursed at them, and Skarde bellowed a warning as did several of his crew.

"To arms! To arms! We are attacked!" he yelled.

He ran down the hull and leapt off the ship to the sandy beach below. The crew formed up in as good an order as could be expected of pirates. Belgeti and his archers were already speeding shafts at their foe. As they called out to rally against the attack, the painted cannibals let out keening war cries. The almost unnatural shrieks straightened the hairs on the back of his neck. *To die in battle is one thing*, he thought, *but the prospect of being eaten afterward is another.*

He ran to the front ranks of his warriors and gripped the pommel of Morsfangsel. He unsheathed the sword and he heard from it a growl in his mind. The cannibals closed in on them, their white and black warpaint ghoulish against their pale pink skin, their hair like wild wings plastered with the same substance they painted their bodies with. Belgeti shouted orders and let an arrow loose with a twang. Again, his archers filled the air with their hissing darts. A dozen fell to the deadly rain, but that did not slow their pace. There were, in his estimate, at least twice as many attackers as his pirates. They tossed javelins at them. A dozen men screamed in pain, and some dropped, but they held ranks.

As the wild mob closed in on them, Skarde felt the spirit of the sword reach out and grasp at his consciousness – for control. *Give me free reign! Lend me your flesh and we shall slay them all!*

Skarde let out a war-cry, as much in defiance of the onrushing foe as to shrug off Morsfangsel's grip on his mind.

"I will slay them all, *myself*!" Skarde roared.

The sword snarled back but gave his hand no resistance as he met the enemy in a clash. He cut a spear in half with his first stroke, and the spearman died a grisly death on the second. Skarde bounded forward and slashed at another opponent, who dodged aside with savage reflexes as sharp as his own. Scowling at Skarde with teeth sharpened to yellowed points, he stabbed at his guts with a stone-tipped spear. Skarde knocked it aside, brought his sword high, and sliced another haft in two. The warrior fled, and another took his place.

As Skarde fought his new foe he jostled shoulders with a compatriot. Their battle line was disrupted, and a wild melee engulfed him. His men were not a trained soldiery, and their opponents even less disciplined. Some kernel of calm rationality in his realized that chaos was inevitable. But his pirates were at the disadvantage even with their superior steel weapons. They were badly outnumbered and soon they would be devoured in a swarm, each man facing multiple opponents.

A second cannibal warrior stabbed at his exposed flank. Skarde swept his sword at his foe's spear, and his supernatural blade sliced through that as well. Pressing his advantage, he roared as he tore in close and arced his weapon at the savage's neck – cutting his head clean from his body. Before the blood-gushing torso toppled, he stabbed at his first foe straight through his guts.

"Back! Back to the ship!" Skarde yelled as he sliced at the air to ward off yet another attacker and sprayed him with gobbets of his own tribesman's blood. "Back and defend!"

Many of the pirates were already withdrawing under the onslaught. Skarde held back half a dozen warriors himself as he directed the crew in something like an orderly retreat. He slashed at hafts thrust at him, and his razor-sharp blade of grey metal broke many. At last, most of his men had scrambled atop the ship's hull. He felt the heavier, wet sand beneath his boots as he neared the ship, but he could not spare even a moment to turn and climb the ropes he knew were only a few paces away without being run through.

Suddenly, he heard a flight whistling death over his head. Feathered shafts sprouted from the guts, chests, and heads of a dozen savages pressing hard in on him, and they collapsed to the beach. His thickly muscled legs bounded back to the ropes in one gigantic leap, and he climbed aboard without dropping his sword. Belgeti and his archers were loosing shaft after shaft, and the brutes below wailed in pain and death.

Atop the tumbled side of the ship's hull, the foe could not easily reach without fighting. The crew, armed with saber and sword, pulled the climbing ropes up after them. The cannibals wailed in rage and anguish as arrow after arrow slew them.

Wailing and shrieking curses in their strange tongue, they ran.

Some turned to hurl a javelin back at the cornered pirates, but none struck true, and those last few attacks cost them even more lives. They fled into the darkening forest and the pirates let out a resounding cheer and held their weapons high in victory. Skarde did so as well, but his face was grim, and his eyes fire!

"We've won!" Bardano exclaimed, his clear voice rising over the others.

"Aye," said Skarde. "We've won – a skirmish. But they are out there, and we are going nowhere."

The men quieted at this and gazed into the trees as the last light of dusk warmed them. Skarde saw no movement, but rather felt the presence of their enemy, and their hate, among the trees. The beach was a red hell. Perhaps fifty of the savages lay unmoving, their blood pooling about them and trickling in rivulets toward the water. Another twenty bodies accounted for their fallen comrades.

"We are strong here," Bardano said after long somber minutes. "If they attack again, we will kill more."

"We'd better collect our arrows," Belgeti said, already scanning for the black and white feathered shafts. "We let many fly and have only a few left."

"Go now," Skarde said, "while there is some light left. I will also go with a few others. We must give our comrades to the sea as high tide goes out. I would prefer to burn or bury them, but we will not have the time."

"We can do it," Bardano said. "We can defeat them!"

Skarde disliked the twinge of panic beginning in Bardano's eyes. "We can!" Skarde said. "Yet, they will return with greater numbers. Who knows how many are out there?"

"We're going to die... and be eaten!" Serigios cried.

"Be silent! You've fought before... why does this place unman you so?" Skarde said.

Serigios paled at the insult and stared off bleakly. "It isn't natural..." he said.

"Maybe not, but these savages bleed. We'll fight our way to Valhalla if nothing else. Now come... let's get to work, and I will think of something."

Chapter Six

"We need to move!" Bardano insisted.

"To the castle?" Eyeboga said. "I do not like the forest. We are better off at sea in a leaking ship."

Serigios shook his head, his eyes wide. He had spoke not a word since Skarde had insulted him, but worked twice as hard with the grim duty of sending their dead to the sea before high tide had left them. "Haunted it is," he said and whether he meant the forest, the castle, or both, he left unspoken.

Skarde had made up his mind before any of the crew had begun to speak. Yet, he wanted to give each man his voice, at least. Perhaps one of them might even concoct some brilliant and unforeseen plan. They had some time before they must needs act, but they had to do something before dawn to his thinking. The cannibals might not come in greater force in the morning – or they might. In either case, Skarde guessed their forces would only grow with time.

"Can we even get into the castle?" Grim-Face asked.

The question was asked before and Skarde sighed. His plan of direct, though desperate, action remained unchanged. Skarde gazed out of the tilted hatch. The gibbous moon peeked now and again through the mists, but for the most part, the suddenly cooling night glowed with an eerie fog. He stood to address his crew.

"We go before dawn. Running through the forest at night will be difficult, but also for our enemy. There is a slope to the north of the castle. My guess is that there is some kind of path that cuts through the escarpment. As for the castle... we have many hooks on ropes for ship grappling. They will serve for scaling walls. Once in, we can negotiate with the inhabitants peacefully, or not so peacefully as the situation demands."

"I can find my footin' through a forest at night!" Hochnay said, his eyes wide with excitement beneath his wild red hair.

"I, too, am undaunted by the forest," Savo said. "The crazed carrot-head and I may guide the others."

Skarde clapped his hands loudly. "You see, we are almost there!"

"But those savages are out there in the forest, no doubt," Grim-Face said. "We won't escape their notice as we cross that beach."

"No," Skarde said. "I have a plan, and with any luck, you will need to fight only a few."

Grim-Face's eyes bulged, and his scarred face gleamed mask-like as he looked on in doubt.

"I intend to leave the ship unseen, by swimming north along the shore," Skarde said. "I'll swim a mile... no more. There, I should be able to crawl up the beach. I will there prowl back through the eaves and slay any savage I encounter."

"Apologies, my Captain," Eyeboga said, polite as ever, "but that plan is madness. You will be slain by a mob."

"A fight is inevitable, and when are odds ever in our favor? I can slay them one on one, and I trust my bushcraft well enough to strike and fade away into the night. I needn't fight all that many. Just enough to cause a ruckus. I intend to draw the main body of brutes northward, leaving a clear path for you. When they come in numbers, it will be easier for one man to evade them than a great number."

"A giant like you, sneak?" said Grim-Face.

Skarde smiled. "I've been a thief when need called. I will not be caught." He tightened his sword belt and scrambled over the debris of their hold. He found a wooden box and pulled from it an ox horn gilt with silver filagree and small red gems, wrapped with a fine leather thong. "The previous captain's finery. Too nice for hard use, but it is what is needed. Gather what food and supplies you can. When you hear a blast from this horn, you will know I have slain one of them. They will come toward me, I hope, as I will make as much a fuss as an army. I hope this will give you what time you need, and... by Thunir's Axe, make your way quick and ungently to the castle. I'll claw and slash my way there, somehow."

They nodded. Wasting no time, Skarde slung the fine horn about his neck and climbed up and out of the slanted stairs, through the hatch, and into the cold night vapors. The moon glowed pale and indistinct like a corpse-light through the fog. Skarde crawled down the askew deck and crept over the rails. He dropped to the sand below with but a single dull thud of his boots. For two score deep breaths, he kept silent and unmoving, his eyes struggling to pierce the shrouded darkness and catch a glimpse of the tree line. He trusted not that the cover of fog and gloom would hide him. He guessed his foe was every bit as savage as he, and their senses supernaturally sharp. At last, he turned and crawled between the hull and the beach, his belly dragging over the sand. He slithered like a snake into the water, warm seeming after the cold air. No sound did he make swimming louder than the gently lapping waves.

For almost an hour, his limbs quietly worked the water. He could have swum faster, but his intention was to be as silent as a catfish. Satisfied that he had rounded whatever company of cannibals had secreted themselves in the forest, he slunk ashore. He slung his sword to his back and crawled along the beach, hardly more than a shadow. They could have scouts even this far out. He would not risk giving himself away. He reached a line of bushes near the trees. His wet skin chilled in the cold air, and his fingertips, sinking into the cool sand, were stiff. He sat on his rump and warmed his hands with his breath for a moment. Then he rose and glided into the dark shadows of the trees.

He drew his sword. He saw no foe, but a shiver in his spine warned against some lurking dread in the forest. He thought of the grim totem of human skulls, the horror of the cannibal's defilement of poor Ilkar, and the strange wraithlike figure. The hysterical warnings of Serigios no longer seemed so foolish.

"Hodan," Skarde whispered, a simple prayer to the All-Father.

He stalked forward with fire in his veins. His eyes sought every contour of shape and shadow, and his feet knew every leaf and twig. No panther could have stalked more silently. The black trunks of the trees drifted past as in a dream. As he journeyed deeper into the woods, he felt as if he had entered a hazy underworld. His footsteps were muffled, but a branch cracking suddenly under his foot was as sharp to his ears as a knife in the back.

A dull orange glow flitted between the black trunks of the trees. He halted, silent as the rocky outcroppings that jutted out of the earth throughout the forest. He gauged where he might be in relation to the ship. Had he crept along a few minutes? An hour? Time seemed immaterial in this strange land. He heard a faint voice, and the crackle of fire. He crept closer, every movement stealth and every footstep planting his toes into the earth like roots. He froze as he caught sight of a face.

A cannibal scanned the darkness, but his eyes flitted unseeing past Skarde. *Has he seen me? No. Soon, it won't matter.* He could just make out five or six figures sitting about a low fire. None of them stared at the fire's glare, but at each other or outward into the night. They had either found or piled up a mound of earth and stones to shield the light from the shore. *Watchers*, Skarde thought. *There might be others. And how many lie nearby, resting for a dawn attack?*

Skarde dropped low and searched the trees. Aside from a few branches near the fire, the trees were an impenetrable black shroud, even in the gloaming mist of the moonlit night. If there were any sentinels in the trees, he wouldn't find them. *Speed*, he thought. *Speed and shock are my weapons. I must put a terror into them.*

He drew his sword, silent as a whisper. The hilt felt suddenly hot, and he knew the cursed blade was eager. He set himself to charge forward, and in a gigantic leap, his mighty thews flung him toward his enemy. As he barreled toward the group, one caught wide-eyed sight of him and snatched up a spear.

Too late. Skarde bellowed a war cry and thrust Morsfangsel into his chest in one smooth motion. He spun and chopped down at the neck of another, nearly decapitating him. As blood spewed from the wrecked body the others wailed in fear and hatred. A javelin darted down from the trees, only just missing him. Skarde seized it up and hurled it at a solid black silhouette in the branches. He saw no body drop, nor heard a scream, but took no further consideration.

"Onward! Onward!" he yelled, and he swung at another cannibal, who scrambled, mad with terror, out of his way.

Skarde dashed out of the dim orange ring of light cast by the fire and ducked behind a tree. He lifted the horn strapped about his neck to his lips and blew a mighty note. The tenor horn resounded through the forest, and Skarde let loose another battle cry. The cannibals hopped to their feet and cried out. Almost twenty figures, as Skarde counted, fled into the night.

"Attack!" Skarde bellowed, and he loosed another blast on the horn with his enormous lungs. "Hordes of the Krigeraknutens be with me!"

He chased after them, thrashing at the branches before him with his sword and roaring enough for a whole pirate crew. He halted for a moment and listened in silence. He could not see his enemy, but he could hear them. Between their shouts, he heard others more distant. They were sounding the alarm, and the tribe was responding. He smiled. His plan was working. *Now, if only I can survive my success.*

He blew his horn again. "Run! Run like beasts before the dragon!"

He could only hope that his men heard his racket, and that enough of the flesh-eating devils would follow him to allow his crew through unseen. He raced forward, sword in hand.

Kill. It was the merest whisper in his mind. The sword. He wondered if it might try to influence him in subtle ways. *Perhaps not. That was not Mor's way in life.*

A shadowy figure darted among the trees only a dozen strides ahead. Had he missed it, he could have been ambushed. He let out a thunderous war cry, blew his horn yet again, and soared forward. There were several figures running before him, just ahead. They leapt off some precipice and disappeared. He rushed forward to another rocky outcropping, and before it an open glade. As the black canopy above him fragmented, the moon, hazy in the thin mist, cast a cold ghostly light down over a wild field. As he topped the rock, he saw five of his quarry scurrying away, and a hundred paces beyond them another six dozen painted warriors crawling through the lissom shadowy grass.

Their skin glowed pallid. Twisted and monstrous seemed their faces and bodies, with flesh bent by the dark paint they wore in slashes and odd curves. Their eyes glittered like baleful stars.

And each one fixed suddenly upon him.

"Luwydi!" Skarde cursed.

They held their spears high and with a wild yell, ran at him. Skarde needed no further spurring. He turned and hopped down, running at a full sprint back into the forest. As the trees blocked out the meager light, Skarde slowed and held the horn to his lips and gave out three short blasts. Did the cannibals need more persuading? A quick glance revealed dozens of forms topping the rise behind him.

Skarde ran as fast as he could through the dense, dark underbrush. A man born of the city would wonder how he moved so swiftly, dodging branches, keeping his feet from tangling in brambles, and avoiding a trip. Skarde was born to woodlands not unlike this one, at the foot of mountains. He flew through the forest on wings of instinct. Over his heaving breath and the crackling branches underfoot, he heard behind him howls of rage and calls for revenge. His swift pursuers, also, were born among the trees.

Now, he almost tumbled out into an open patch. To either side, he sensed a clear route. In an instant, he chose to run along the path. Though it led him sidelong before his oncoming foe, he could sprint as he could not in the heavy brush. Counting on his long, powerful strides to disentangle himself from his current situation, he ran as he had never run before. One after the other dark shapes crashed through the trees to his right. He was just ahead of their band. He heard shouts behind him, and he knew they were on the same path, all too close. *Must I run all the way to the castle?* His legs burned but his savage heart yearned to turn and fight.

Yes. Turn and let us fight! Open yourself to me. Together, we have the power to kill them all!

The damnable sword, he thought. A rage grew in him. Was it caused by the sentient sword that imprisoned the spirit of the giant, Mor, that kindled his ire? Or perhaps he was but angered that the cursed blade could reach out to his mind so easily.

"Nay, you bastard!" he grunted between breaths. Yet the thought of acceding to the sword, and turning to fight, did flit through his skull.

He ran all the harder. Few men were as tireless as he, but sprinting over rough ground in this murk was exhausting. He was far ahead of his hunters, and so allowed himself a lesser pace to conserve his strength. The canopy of trees opened up here and there, and wan fingers of moonlight stretched downward to illuminate the path. In a patch of such light, a dark form moved. He slowed to a jog. In the mist and strange light, he imagined he saw a man and the glimmer of eyes, yet the thing moved oddly. Was a man crawling toward him? Unwilling to slow, Skarde swung his sword with a cry.

His sword thunked into something solid, like flesh. The form let out a horrific squeal. In a baffling movement, the thing split in two, behind where he had struck it. The injured party flung itself to the side of the trail, and the other let out an inhuman grunt and launched itself at him. Hard bone cracked into Skarde's knee with a shock of pain. He tumbled heels over head to the side of the trail. In an instant, the black form pounced on him and bit his leg. In a cacophonous fury, it shook his limb. Skarde swung down and struck the thing with his sword. It let out a deafening squeal and fled into the bush.

Wincing, Skarde laughed. "Boars! I fought two boars! Damn my eyes. There is a curse on this place!"

He stood. At least no bone was broken, though he could see his breeches were torn to rags. He moved forward at with limp and a dull throbbing. His left leg was injured. T the tribe of flesh-eaters wailed and hooted not far enough away behind him.

"Damn. I've no time for pain," he said.

He began to run. His leg ached, but he gritted his teeth and kept going. Still, his effort was in vain. He limped forward, slower and unsteady every time his left foot hit the ground. He could bear the suffering, but he just could not move fast enough. He halted and weighed the sword in his hand, looking back down the path. The cannibals would be on him soon.

Aye! The sword whispered.

Skarde shut his mind to the bloodthirsty blade. *Will it make a slave of me if I give in? There is no telling.* He glanced to the southeast. He could not see the castle through the trees, but the split peaks of the mountain loomed above. He must be more than halfway there. The trail turned eastward. *If I must move slowly, why not slow the enemy as well...* He dove into the forest northward, taking as direct a path to the castle as he could guess.

He delved through the deep brush, hoping his sudden course change would shake his pursuers. *Bah, fool, hope is a poor bet against devils.* He sped on hellbent against the pain and the sloping ground. Bare stone shimmered in moonlight that peeked through the silver limned clouds. Perhaps the changeable gods of this land were watching this spectacle unfold. A quick glance at his leg revealed it was bloody, but the injury was not deep.

Skarde climbed over one rocky ledge after another. The already thinning trees stopped altogether, and he was faced with a towering rock wall. He paused to listen. Behind him, the forest crackled with twigs breaking underfoot and whooshed with branches thrust aside.

"No rock has daunted me yet," Skarde said. "Let's see how well these savage bastards can climb."

He slid his sword back into its scabbard, and he felt on the edge of his consciousness that it was offended. He ran up the steepening slope until he needed to grip the rough rock in his fingers. Finding a foothold, and then another, he lifted himself upward. His leg grieved him as he climbed, but it obeyed. He grazed his shin on a sharp edge and his lips stiffened at the sting. In the moonlight, he saw a few drops of blood still flowed and fell downward.

His eyes were drawn from his dripping blood to the sight of the cannibals beneath him. A few launched javelins at him, but they fell short, clattering off the rock face. He laughed and turned his head over his shoulder to taunt them.

"I am your king! See – you imps are all beneath me!"

If they could not understand his tongue, they understood the tone. They jeered back at him, and as stragglers from the forest chase filled out their ranks, they, too, began to climb.

"Nine Hells!" Skarde said.

He hastened his climb. His left leg ached with every push off, but he preferred that to being eaten. As he lifted himself above the tops of the tall trees a ruddy glow lit the torn shreds of iron grey clouds. Looking down the sheer rock face, he saw that some of the tribe were quicker than others. One of the bastards was only five paces below him. He pulled himself up, crag by crag, at a reckless pace. Skarde put to work every bit of talent he had picked up climbing as a child in his rocky homeland. The light increased and, at last, he topped the cliff face, a sheer rocky shelf of several hued layers.

Beautiful, he thought. Perhaps even more so in light of the immediate threat, but also fleeting. He took no time to take in the magnificent vista but picked up a heavy stone and hurled it down the precipice at his impetuous pursuer.

The cannibal dodged aside, but the rock caught his arm. It made a dull cracking sound and he screamed as he lost his grip and tumbled down a hundred paces to be dashed upon the hard slope below. The painted savage's descent almost dislodged another, but he somehow hung on with a desperate hold and regained his footing.

"I won't see you all off by hurling stones," Skarde said, "so I will leave you with the blessings of Luwydi."

He ran to the south along a path of stone slabs and broken turf. His leg numbed, though he would have welcomed the pain back if it meant he could move more quickly. Though he still sprinted faster than most men could, that limb seemed to drag. Trees lined the cliff face a few paces away, and some clung tenaciously to its very edge. Soon, the savages would top the escarpment in a wide front. He thought to get ahead of them before they clambered up, but drew his sword should any of them surprise him. The sun rose behind the mountains, lighting the sky in a hazy orange glow. He glanced behind. They were only now scrambling over the edge, but he was not as far ahead as he would have liked.

A single high tower of the castle now stood in view away off to the south-east. He hobbled on. The forest about him thickened, and he crashed through branches heedless of scratches and buffets. The flesh-eaters were right behind him, though now, he dared not look for fear of missing a single step.

Sunlight began to pierce the haze and a brightness lay ahead. The forest came to a sudden end, and the castle lay some three hundred strides away. He flew past hundreds of tree stumps in the thinning mists. It seemed to cling to the rocky ledge like the gravity defying trees he had passed. Before him was a rough road rutted with eroded wagon tracks. It led from the castle to just a score of paces in from the treeline. Here it turned west into the steep slope that broke through the cliff face. He ran along it toward a crenelated grey wall of stone which teetered upon the very edge of the precipice and swooped over to a rounded tower. Behind that stood a small inner keep with one tall tower lording over all beneath it. He saw no guard or sign of activity and was prepared to climb the sheer wall if even a hundred men stood atop with bows.

Like a roll of thunder, a roar swept over him. He glanced back and cannibals issued from the treeline like a swarm of wasps. Dozens charged at him, spears held high, javelins at the ready, and faces twisted by rage. They rushed at him with such madness that seemed desperate to him. With a curse, he sprinted over the rough ground and ignored the agony in his leg. He sped forward less quickly than he liked, and he expected some attack.

Looking for a spot to climb the walls, he saw the castle surrounded by a steep rocky slope that met a ravine. Suddenly, a figure popped up upon the battlements.

Skarde stood mouth agape, eyes wide to see it was Belgeti.

He gesticulated and shouted madly, and Skarde grasped that he should come about the castle to its east side. A dozen of Belgeti's own archers rose from behind the crenels and knocked arrows. Skarde raced to the rocky ravine. It meandered in and curved about the outcrop the castle was seated on. Down its tumultuous slopes was a narrow, roaring river that led to a waterfall. It was only fifteen feet wide but rushing wild.

Skarde halted for frantic heartbeat to consider his descent when he glanced back at the cannibals. They had stopped dead in their tracks, having crossed only half of the distance between the forest edge and the castle walls. He glanced about. Was this a ruse? Were there some coming at him from his side or from behind? He saw none.

With the spark of madness known only to berserkers lit inside him, he laughed. Raising his sword he belted out a challenge. "Come, dogs and taste death!"

"Skarde!" Belgeti barked. "No time to make friends. Come inside! The way is open."

Skarde shrugged and looked about one last time, expecting some surprise. He turned to Belgeti and nodded. The road led around a mound of stone and, to his shock, an open drawbridge. It spanned the space over the river which snaked right around the base of the castle.

Hodan's beard! How did they get the castellan to open up so quickly, he wondered? As he stepped forward, his hair stood on end, and eerie sense of uncanny wrongness put a cold stone in his stomach. The misty air carried a hint of charnel stench, no longer sickening but enough to set his teeth on edge. There, at the foundation of the bridge, was a body. Step by step he edged forward over the creaking wooden crossing, and a gut-wrenching vista opened to him. Some hundred dead bodies lay scattered about the courtyard. Slumped and flattened, Skarde saw blackened flesh and exposed bones where they were not covered by cloth or recently tarnished armor. He froze and gazed over the scene of horror, his eyes wide beneath taut brows.

Chapter Seven

"It wasn't us," Belgeti said.

Skarde turned his bulging eyes from the hoary slaughter in the courtyard to the furious cannibals in the distance. They hadn't moved much, except to spread out. Soon they would surround the castle, and Skarde and his men would find themselves besieged. Dashing up a flight of stone steps, he mounted the wall, and Belgeti followed. From their vantage point upon the battlements, he could see further into the forest. Here and there he caught sight of a savage warrior flitting between the trees. The horror inside the walls became clearer as well, but questions crowded Skarde's mind.

"No, of course it wasn't us," Skarde said, finally answering Belgeti. "The bodies are some months rotted."

"It would seem evident. Yet I must say it, nonetheless. This place stinks not only of bodies, but of the uncanny," Belgeti said. "What powers of *Tomog*..."

Skarde did not doubt his judgment, but he pressed his friend. "Oh, why?"

"Do you not feel it? The men feel it. Look upon their faces. Serigios..."

Skarde looked for his once stout mason and pirate. The legend of the place had rattled him. Now, he stood alone, his back to the wall of the keep. His shoulders slumped and his eyes darted to and fro. *Like a man whose nerves are frayed before a battle*, Skarde thought.

"Aye, I feel something...," Skarde said. "Why is the drawbridge down?"

"We found it so, only a little while before you came," Belgeti said. "My blood fired when I saw it, and I thought some trap was set for us. But as we entered, my heart suddenly chilled."

"I had hoped for a welcoming cheer, if I lived, but I will not hold the uneasy silence of the men against them. I am most uneasy about our flesh-eating friends out there. Why? Why have they not attacked?"

"Perhaps they fear my bowmen?" Belgeti said with a cynical snort.

Skarde eyed him. "The slaughter is a grim sight, but the cold earth awaits us all. That, the Gods deem natural. But why do those warriors not attack? Look – they are returning to the trees. Do they fear the same uncanny presence you feel?" Skarde shivered at the thought.

Belgeti only nodded.

"Come," Skarde said, "let us look into one mystery before all else. The drawbridge."

Skarde walked along the crenellated wall and through a round tower at the south side of the gate. He pressed on the wooden door, which swung open with a creak. He wrinkled his nose as he was hit with the stench of death.

"Pah!" he choked. "This place needs an airing."

Belgeti nodded, his face twisted in displeasure.

With an act of will, Skarde stepped in. Two corpses lay upon the floor beside the winch mechanism. Belgeti choked as he lifted his hand to his mouth. They approached the bodies. One was a man armored in chain. His head had an odd shape to it. Belgeti cleared his throat and plucked an arrow from his quiver. With the tip, he pressed into the man's mop of black hair. Though the decayed body was dry, Belgeti curled his lip in disgust as the cracked leather of its scalp flaked. The skull beneath was cut and pressed apart in a cracking line.

Skarde caught Belgeti's eyes and knew without a word that they shared the thought – murder. Skarde glanced over at the other body. He wore a leather jerkin and shirt of white wool, now stained with months of neglect and dried blood. He held in his hand a forester's knife, and not far away lay an axe. The blade of the axe was crusted black and brown with rust and gore.

Skarde noticed that the ropes about the winch had been hacked, and their frayed ends were also stained with long dried blood. The forester's knife was befouled much like the axe, though it still lay clenched in the decayed hand. Belgeti bend to look over the body and tugged at the jerkin on the corpse's torso with his arrow.

"He holds his knife turned up, not aligned with his knuckles," Skarde said. "Check his neck."

Belgeti flashed wide eyes at Skarde before bending low and prodding at his throat.

"His skin is like frail, rotted black leather... it is hard to see. No, I see it. It does look like his throat is cut."

"Snakes of P'thon! That is a grim tale. I can not read it any other way," Skarde said.

"Murder, sabotage, and suicide," Belgeti said. "But why?"

Skarde's mind groped for an answer. He turned and gazed out through an arrow slit at the treeline beyond. Mist still curled in serpent-like forms at the roots of the trees, and Skarde sneered. "Why? Men do mad things. Who can say?"

"Let's go," Belgeti said, sounding defeated. "Perhaps some reason will present itself as we explore the castle."

"Where the mind errs, feet must do," Skarde said.

A second door lay to the south, and they took it. They walked the walls, investigated the towers, and surveyed the grounds. It was much like any other castle, and besides the massacre and murder, nothing seemed amiss. There were stables, but no horse, living or dead, occupied it. To the west were terraces, lower than the courtyard, and hanging, it seemed, over the very edge of the cliff.

Skarde leaned on the wall and gazed down hundreds of feet to the rocky slope beneath. Could the savages have scrabbled sidelong across the crags and climbed the low wall? They might have, but even a handful of defenders could have fought off an army of climbers, pushing them one after the other to a winged death. He gazed out over the sylvan vista, and for a moment, forgot his dilemma. The forest below, shrouded in mist, was beautiful but held a threat of some unfathomable secret. Beyond that, the ocean lay. It called to him with a song of freedom and adventure. His mind wandered, and he invented reasons to explain the unexplainable.

"Faeries, giants, or trolls... which do you suppose more likely taught these savage men their flesh-eating ways?"

"They took turns, no doubt," Belgeti said.

Skarde laughed, put aside his speculation, and they continued their exploration. On the lowest terrace, on the south-west corner of the castle, stood a heavy stone-built arch. Skarde stuck his head in. A dark tunnel ran upward to another arch some ways off. The air here was cold and damp. It chilled his barbarian intuition as well, and sent a shiver of ghostly fear across his skin.

Skarde set his jaw and entered, his eyes darting. They found a heavy iron-bound door in the wall. Skarde pushed at it, but it was sturdy and immobile. He shrugged and followed the tunnel back up to the courtyard where their men waited anxiously. Of the keep, no other door or means of ingress was found open to them. Skarde eyed it with suspicion. He called the whole crew of some seventy men to listen. When they had assembled, he spoke.

"Belgeti and I have found that the gate room you see above was breached. Some saboteur cut the ropes to the drawbridge, permitting the attack that occurred here months ago. Nothing else have we found about the castle grounds."

"What of the keep itself?" asked Hochnay.

Skarde turned to eye it, and then back at Hochnay. "Still a mystery. There are but two doors – one off the tunnel and the main entry before us here in the courtyard. Both are locked and very sturdy. There are no windows save these arrow loops, and no man could slip through them."

"Might we climb the tower?" Bardano asked.

"I might manage it with the grappling hooks... if you brought some."

"We brought them all," Belgeti said.

"And our supplies?"

"We have enough food for a week. A little more if we eat light," Belgeti said.

"And enough water for a few days," Eyeboga interjected. "Though the water from the stream in the little ravine appears clean enough."

"We don't want to go out to fetch any, if we can help it," Skarde said. "Speaking of coming and goings, we must fix the drawbridge with all haste."

"Why?" Said Hochnay. "The bastards do not approach the castle. It's as if they fear it."

"Aye," Skarde said. "But I would put my trust in a thick gate over a scarecrow. Who knows what scared our friends out there, and what might bring them sudden bravery?"

"So, you think they will leave us be in a few days?" Eyeboga asked. His voice hinted at hope.

"Ach, nay!" Hochnay barked. "These savages have it out for us."

Eyeboga stared crossly at Hochnay, then turned back with a pleading look. Skarde nodded at Hochnay to Eyeboga's dismay. "These are savage men. More savage than Hochnay, more savage than I. They do not think of profit and danger like a city man might. To them, we are intruders. They may have even mistaken us for reinforcements for this lot," Skarde swept his hand at the corpses about courtyard.

"Why don't we ask them nicely to leave?" Grim-Face said. There was a dark chuckle under his breath.

"Aye," Skarde said. "Go ask them as we repair the drawbridge."

Grim-Face's ghastly smile did nothing to boost the morale of the men.

"Come. We have much to do." Skarde named a few men with the cleverest hands to repair the front gate, and the rest, he led in disposing of the bodies. Appalled but determined, they lifted the dried cadavers on to a few spare cloaks. Then, down the stairs to the first terrace they went. No men took the darkened tunnel to the lower second terrace, even if the bodies were closer to its mouth. 'There's a chill, unwholesome air down it,' many said.

They had few options. Skarde intended to simply toss the bodies over the ramparts. *An unfitting burial*, he lamented, *but what else can we do*? He wondered if the ghosts of the soldiers might haunt them for the offense but kept the thought to himself. He led the grim procession, carrying a dried blackish husk with Farasid. The body weighed less than he made it out to be, much of it from the chainmail. They tossed the carcass over the side and returned up the stair, passing the grim procession, to retrieve another. Skarde was surprised, as they hauled their second body, to find that no one was returning up the stairs.

When they set foot on the first terrace, they saw several bodies laid out on the ground in a row. Skarde's eyes widened as he saw the pirates rifling through the personal affects of the dead. Some were inspecting coin purses; others were pulling rings from fingers; one had removed the tarnished but serviceable chainmail and was shaking it out with a rattle. Farasid dropped the body to the ground and sprang up.

"Despoilers!" Farasid barked.

Skarde turned his attention to his colleague. He had one hand settled upon his sword. Skarde stepped in front of him in alarm, recalling that Farasid had lost his brother Kasuk only a few months ago. *For him to see the dead plundered must bring up hard memories*, Skarde thought, *still, I can't allow a fight among my men, particularly now.*

"Hold, Farasid!" he said. "Come with me a moment, back up the stairs."

Farasid, his face somewhat ashen, tightened his fist upon his hilt.

"There will be no fight here now," Skarde said. "Unless it be with me."

Clenching his jaw, Farasid nodded, and released his pommel. He turned and stiffly walked up the stairs.

"It must be hard," Skarde said. "I guess what pain is in you... but I ask, is it not better to steal from the dead than from the living?"

Farasid took a deep breath and spoke not, though Skarde could see the thoughts whirling through his head in his sad eyes.

"We are thieves, no? Brigands of the sea? These men have no need of their earthly possessions. Their armor might turn a deadly blow for one of us, and a few coins jangling in a purse on their belts might give them an ounce of hope. Forgive their small sacrilege," he said, holding up thumb and finger to denote a pinch. "Let them have their small treasures."

"Of course, captain... I was overcome," Farasid said, hanging his head low.

"Perhaps you should assist in securing the front gate? That is needed with all haste. You are a handy enough fellow."

"Of course, Captain," he said.

He turned and left before Skarde could say more. When he had topped the stairs and disappeared, Skarde dragged the body to the edge. *Farasid near cracked just now, Serigios has a mad look to him, and Bardano and Eyeboga are stricken with grief over Ilkar, though they show it little. Who else is at their wits end that I do not see? Things will go badly if I cannot devise a plan to improve our lot... but what might I do? Hells! By Luwydi, may our luck improve.*

Chapter Eight

"Fine work," Skarde said, clapping Eyeboga on the back. With the drawbridge retracted and closed tight the men would feel more at ease.

Eyeboga dipped his head gracefully. "The winch was in good enough condition."

"How swiftly might we open and close it?"

"With our strongest men at the winch? Perhaps two minutes, maybe less.

"Hmm," Skarde brooded. "Let us lower it and try for half that."

Eyeboga's eyebrows raised. "We've just got the castle secured and you wish to open it?"

"We won't be staying long, friend, if I can help it."

"Do you have a plan, Captain?"

"No, but I am brewing one in my skull. Go and gather Bardano, Hochnay, Grim-Face, and Savo and meet in the winch room. I will get Belgeti."

Eyeboga nodded and set off at a stiff pace to gather them. Skarde climbed the wooden steps to the wall top and approached Belgeti. He stood with him for a moment surveying the treeline.

"Have the sentries seen anything?" Skarde said.

"Oh yes," Belgeti smiled. "A few rabbits; a fox; one or two cannibals."

"Do you think you and your archers could put a pin in one?"

Belgeti shook his head. "They stay among the trees. I might get an arrow out that far, high arcing. But to hit a mark in the trees? Doubtful."

"Perhaps if they came closer... or you went closer to them?"

"A sortie?"

"Maybe," Skarde said. "I am wondering aloud. Come, we will talk with a few others."

Skarde led his friend along the wall. As they entered the wooden room above the gate, none noticed a dark figure slink away from an arrow slit near the top of the high square tower. Inside, the gathered crew eyed Skarde in anticipation.

Skarde took a deep breath and smiled. "It seems to me our plans have not much changed. Only that the wheel has come off our apple cart."

"You liken our situation to an apple cart? We are surrounded by cannibals!" Savo said.

"Well," Skarde said, "that is how we started when we beached the ship, though we did not know it. Eyeboga, how much longer would you need to work on the ship – just to get it to sail a few dozen miles down coast?"

"With enough men... aye, I could nail down a few boards more and use a tarp and some pitch to plug the holes. A few hours. We would need the tide to push out though."

Skarde nodded. "Perhaps we could manage that."

"They will kill us if we leave the castle," Grim-Face said. "I still wonder why they did not follow us."

"The captain distracted them once, why not again? I also volunteer to go and give them a rattle." Bardano shook the sword at his side and gave Skarde an eager smile.

"Aye," Skarde said. "I thought Hochnay and myself might cause such a tumult, along with a few eager lads. You are wood-crafty, no?"

Hochnay smiled. "I could swim through the earth and pop up to stab them in their backsides. They've no idea what a Commorian can do!"

"This seems wild and unlikely," Savo said.

"Savo, do not be so glum! We are halfway to a plan," Skarde said. "There is one other advantage we have."

"Go on," Savo said as Skarde paused dramatically.

"The terraces of the castle hang over the cliffs. We have enough rope to make a line that would reach the bottom. We could sneak the whole crew down if we had enough time, though I imagine we would be caught. What if two or three men hung from a line and, say, ten of us lowered them all at one go?"

Savo considered it, but Eyeboga's eyes widened at the prospect.

"Think on it, dogs," Skarde said. "We could try this, mayhap, tomorrow evening after we've all rested well and gained all our strength back."

Savo, Eyeboga and the rest nodded in agreement, though each one knew they were in the hands of the Gods. *The Fates weave our destiny*, Skarde thought, *but mayhap we might put our own hands on the loom and shake it 'til it rattles.*

As Skarde hobbled out to the wall, Belgeti caught his arm. Skarde turned and caught his questioning eye. "Eh," Skarde said, though Belgeti's look spoke that he should al know. "What is it?"

"That is a bold plan for a wobbly leg. It's time you let me bandage it and take a rest."

"There is much to do," Skarde said.

"Aye, and it will get done slower with you limping. I'll get a chair and you can sit quiet and watch for ghosts and man-devils as I patch you up," Belgeti said.

"You are a rude nurse-maid." Skarde said.

The men took the rest of the day at a slow pace. Some organized the baubles taken from the deceased defenders as Skarde had ordered equal shares for all. Some kept their minds busy and played at games and gambling. Little of the enemy was sighted, but all the men, Skarde included, felt a brooding menace beyond the walls.

Twilight came, and Skarde ordered the gate lowered. As soon as it kissed the ground, they reversed and closed it. Skarde was satisfied, if not impressed, at their speed.

"A man might cover the distance from the forest to the castle gate in less time, but the rough ground, the rocky ravine, and the river would make the run much more difficult," he said.

Then, he had it lowered halfway – just enough for a man to squeeze out. Sentries kept close watch on the darkling skulkers under limb and leaf. Skarde and Bardano stood at either side of the opening, sword in hand and eyes open for any surprises. A few men slipped outside and skittered down the rocky slope to the river to fill up their waterskins. There was never enough supply in a siege, and Skarde hoped to fill every container they could find. Other men departed for the terraces, where the treasure, weapons, armor, and clothing had been doffed from the previous defenders. A few men came lugging chainmail and weapons they intended to clean.

"Can't blame them for wanting to wash the decay of the dead away," Bardano said after the small gang had climbed through the half open portal.

"Aye," Skarde said. "And daring to go outside the castle walls – a bold act inspires confidence."

"To triumph over..." Bardano's rejoinder was cut off by screams and a clash of weapons. "That came from inside the walls!"

"Nine Hells! You men by the river! In! Now!" Skarde bellowed. He ran back, limping on his bandaged leg, and looked up at the window in the winch room. "As soon as they are inside, close the gate!"

Skarde continued hobbling around the castle with Bardano close at his heels. Grim-Face charged up the stairs from the first terrace, sword in hand and eyes wide.

"Captain, we've been attacked!"

"Lead on!" Skarde said.

Skarde jumped down the stairs after Grim-Face, taking them in two massive strides despite the pain. There, in the middle of the terrace lay four of his men in a growing pool of blood. One lay on the stones, gripping his right breast, his face a mask of pain. He was coddled by another, and five more pirates stood bewildered, with their swords drawn.

"We came down as soon as we heard the brawl and found this," Grim-Face said.

"Damn!" Skarde said. He hobbled over to the injured man and knelt down. "Abakar! What happened?"

Abakar looked up at Skarde and drew a pained breath. "They came flying up the stairs on a frozen wind, their black cloaks fluttering! They wailed and blades like ice cut us down! Wraiths! That's what they were, wraiths!"

Skarde's eyes flashed wide. Despite his injury, Abakar told his tale with a bitter, cutting voice. Men watching from over the wooden balustrade gazed on in fear. Suddenly, one of their number shrieked madly and ran off.

For a moment, all stood watching with stunned faces.

"Nine Hells! It's Serigios! After him, he's gone mad!" Skarde said.

Bardano took that command to heart and flew up the stairs, followed by a few others. Skarde turned back to Abakar and tugged at his blood-soaked jerkin. A bloody stab wound gaped high on his chest near his shoulder.

"You aren't hacking up blood," Skarde said. "You might live. I'll get Belgeti..."

"Captain!" A man from the court yelled. "Serigios flew like a bat out of the gate!"

"Luwydi! What strange mood came over me to ask you for favors!" He said as he sprang up and moved as fast as his leg would allow up the stairs.

A small crowd had gathered at the gate, but Skarde cleared a path. He leapt through the wide crack between the half-raised drawbridge and the wall and landed on his left leg with a painful thud. Bardano was half-way through the opening, but Skarde issued a sharp command for him to remain. As Skarde turned to pursue, Serigios had already topped the other side of the ravine. He flew heedless down the rough road that would meet the drawbridge when down. North the road wend and turned eastward about an outcrop of many layered rock.

"Halt! Fool!" Skarde cried aloud.

He clambered down the rocky slope and splashed through the rapid flow of the river. Gritting his teeth, he climbed the other side and limped as fast as most men could run. The scent of the cool humid forest filled his nose. Tendrils of fog crept from the eaves as if it sensed an approaching victim . The skin of his leg felt tight like the canvas of a tent in a windstorm. Generally, he would have had no problem catching the older, shorter man. Skarde willed himself to fly onward. Serigios had almost reached the trees, and the road turned southward down a gentler slope – the only break in the escarpment. A glance revealed that Bardano was but a hundred paces behind him. *Damn! We'll all be those savages' dinner!*

"Halt!" Skarde bellowed. "Bardano! Your captain commands!"

At that, Bardano slowed. He shouted at Serigios as he disappeared down the slope. Skarde turned to catch him and threw his arms about him roughly. He dragged Bardano to a stop.

"Captain! They'll get him!" Bardano protested.

"They've got him, and they'll get us," Skarde's voice strained through clenched teeth. "They are but allowing us to get closer. Come away!"

"Captain, we can still…" Bardano's pleading was cut short by thundering war cries.

Five or six dozen painted cannibals flew from under the darkening trees, perhaps guessing that the two would come no closer. Bardano, at once, put off trying to fight against Skarde. They both turned, and the pair raced back toward the castle. He willed the agony in his leg to take its toll later, and the cannibals gave up their thundering war cry to sprint at their victims. As they quieted, Skarde heard a piercing scream of agony in the distance.

Serigios has found his end.

Skarde knotted his brows. Rage and grief filled his eyes, but the clatter of javelins biting the gravel at their feet told again of their pressing need to flee. *What I would give to slay all these bastards*, he thought. Morsfangsel, in his hand, answered with a prickling sensation up his arm. From here, the top of the castle's walls was visible over the rock outcrop. Ten men thereabouts stood upon them, the bows they held just slender black lines against a dimming grey sky.

Arrows hissed overhead and several savages cried out in agony. Another volley sliced the air, and by then, Skarde and Bardano had turned the kink in the road. Skarde glanced back. Again, the cannibals had retreated to the trees. *The archers*, Skarde thought, *are not why the savages have turned tail.* The pair scrambled down and up the river's ravine and climbed through the half-closed gate.

"Shut it!" Skarde cried.

He hardly needed to give the order. Men were already pulling the cranks hard, and the door creaked upward and shut with a wooden thud. Every man's face was turned toward him. They awaited his word – some hoping for some miraculous report that Serigios had somehow lived. Skarde surveyed the faces. Most looked on, simply awaiting confirmation of what they already knew. Skarde glared back, every bit as grim.

"Set a watch on the walls, and a watch at both ends of the tunnels." He said in a flat voice, like one expecting an attack from an unknown quarter.

"Shouldn't we flee this accursed place?" Savo said. "I'd feel safer back at the ship. Didn't you plan to climb down the cliff with ropes?"

"I planned to send a handful down the ropes," Skarde said. "How many lines might we knot together? Two? Three if we are very lucky. Each line might take two men safely. Nay. It would take us hours to escape the castle that way and split our strength in half at that. We stay in the castle, at least for a spell. The cannibals fear it."

"Aye. They fear those wraiths!" Savo said. "What chance do we have against supernatural horrors?"

The men grumbled in agreement, though none seemed particularly keen on leaving the protection of the walls either.

"Aye... supernatural." Skarde said. "Stick together, men, and we shall be secure enough."

"But captain," Savo said, "you don't know..."

"No more chatter!" Skarde barked. "Do you challenge me? I am captain, and my word is final. If you wish to try your luck outside the walls, go now and spare us your doubts!"

"Nay, captain. I will stay," Savo said, eyes cast down.

Skarde nodded. "We will unearth all spooks, specters, and goblins tomorrow. 'Til then, we all stay together in the courtyard and keep a watch."

"Aye," the men called, though their voices were disheartened.

Chapter Nine

The morning brought no cheer to the men. Mist climbed the castle walls and crawled over the crenels like ghostly fingers. The sky was like billowing lumps of cold iron. Clouds loomed over them as grey headed storm giants, threatening, but holding back the onslaught for the moment.

Skarde ate. No one spoke to him, though few said any words at all. Feeling as grim as the sky above, he took two grappling hooks from the store of goods the men had taken from the ship, and limped about the castle down the stairs to the first terrace on the west side.

Here, he marked his best chances of climbing the wall. He eyed an arrow slit and gauged its distance and angle. He spun a hook about and tossed it up, missing his mark by several feet. It clanged off the surface and rattled against the stone ground. He tried again and again. The shot was difficult with the narrow opening some forty feet straight up. He had the time.

Belgeti came and stood nearby, calmly watching each attempt. Skarde glanced at him with furled brows. At last, the hook tumbled inside the slit, and held tight as he tugged at it. He smiled like he had slain a foe.

"Are you sure you won't take men with you?" Belgeti asked. "You may need a few dozen swords."

Skarde shook his head, in no mood to argue. "It there were a garrison in there, they would have come out to slaughter us already. If there is a ghost, no one will go in."

"I will come, and Bardano too. He would be only too glad to get a chance to impress you."

Skarde ground his teeth. The young man was not unlike himself but a few years ago; eager to show his colors, eager for the favour of his leaders. *And where have I led him?*

"Bardano is cracking. Much evil has befallen him, and he might go to fey extremes to impress me. And you..." Skarde said, "you are the only sane man left among us."

"Truly, we are doomed," Belgeti laughed.

Skarde smiled. "If I die, get them out of here."

"If it is a ghost, what will you do?" Belgeti asked.

"Stick it with my sword. It has a ghost of sorts in it. And maybe the blow will rid me of both."

"If the sword is such a burden, toss it over the side," said Belgeti.

"You don't hold with Sulmei's warning? No, the blade will call out to man or beast to use. I have heard its whispers in my mind and won a battle of wills. But it still hates me and would have revenge. Better that I wield it until some means of being rid of it forever is brought to light."

Belgeti nodded as Skarde tied the end of the rope of the second grapple about his waist. He pulled himself up. Thick muscles strained in his arms and back. Halfway up his foot slipped across the stones wetted by the mists. His bandaged leg tumbled against the rough stone. Clenching his jaw, he righted himself and was thankful his injury was not deep.

He clambered his way to the arrow slit. He pulled himself up to peek in. It was dismally dark inside. Steep stairs turned around an inner wall. There was a sconce with a withered black torch, long since exhausted.

Wrapping the taut rope about his wrist, he clung to it with one hand and hauled the second hook up. Twenty feet above him was the top of the square tower. He whirled the hook and released it. He had a much easier target despite his awkward position, and the hook flew over the edge on his first shot. He pulled it back and after a tug, it seemed secure enough. Releasing his wrist from the first line, he swung to the side of the tower and back. After coming to a rest, he hauled himself up and over the parapet.

He drew his sword right away, though the tower landing was clear. It had but one entry – a dark wooden trap door with a rough wooden handle. Skarde pulled the door open and stepped back lest he be met with a missile. No such attack came. Beneath him was a wooden ladder wrapped with rope. Water dripping through the trap door had darkened the wood, but it proved solid as he put his weight upon it and descended.

He found himself at the top of a stone stairwell. A shadow filled hall ran along the length of the keep. The smell of moisture and mildew filled the air. He crinkled his nose and sniffed. He smelled a faint trace of hearth smoke. *How long ago was a fire lit within these walls?*

With utmost care, he crept down the hall with doors set on one side. The heavy boards did not creak but even the leather of his boots seemed a lawless intrusion in the heavy silence. Stopping before the first door, he pressed in on it, cautiously but robustly. The door felt solid and did not budge. He was determined to sniff out every square inch of the place, but was unwilling to make noise just yet. In the back of his mind, he weighed the idea of getting his men to help smash down the door. He left it and padded to the second door halfway down the hall.

That door swung open with a creak that set his teeth on edge. In it was a large bed, expertly made but unadorned. No tapestries hung on the wall as he had seen in other fortifications, but crude furs. He padded over to a wardrobe, again well made but simple. Reaching out, he pulled it open. It was filled with women's clothing of the style of Saraylos. He dropped low and peeked under the bed. Nowhere in the room could he find any living person, but the place seemed lived in. His uncivilized instincts sensed something amiss; a thrill of danger flew down his spine.

He crept about that level, slow and steady like a spider on the hunt, but no further sign of recent occupancy did he find among the spartan décor. Next, he tried the slender stairs, almost too narrow for his massive shoulders. He found a single room with dozens of narrow beds and more bedrolls. At the far end were tables covered in cups and plates. The furniture was, as in the room above, sturdy and simple. Skarde raised an eyebrow at the sight of a crossbow sitting upon a bed beside an arrow slit. It was cocked, bolt secured and ready to fly. Beside it was a small cloth roll. Skarde picked it up and sniffed it. His eyes widened, stung by the scent of a strong cheese Southerners loved. He unrolled it. He found a small roll of bread, and cheese half eaten.

The rafters above him creaked.

Skarde froze. For long minutes he waited, the sharp edge of his senses reaching out through the gloom. Listening. Waiting. He hardly dared to breathe. No other noise came, save a low moan of wind and a scuffle from the gloomy men outside. Could it have been the wind creaking the timbers?

Skarde inspected the tables. Here, there were dozens of wooden dishes and cups. He found no sign of food or drink, hardly a dried stain or desiccated scrap. Skarde conjured images of men rushing from a meal to defend their castle, never to return – only to have someone later clean their plates. *Did the cannibals invade the keep? Surely, they would have torn the place to shreds... I like this not.*

He moved toward the door to the staircase in the square tower and heard whispering. It was faint and went as quickly as it came. His palms tingled. He looked at his sword. *Was it you, you cursed thing?*

The sword made no reply. For the moment it seemed as dead and cold as the strange metal it was forged of.

His sense of unease grew. The walls seemed to shrink in on him. His mind wandered as he listened for any sign of a trap. *What was the purpose of this castle in the savage wildlands? What happened months ago, just before the slaughter? Why do the savages fear to come in?* He shook the thoughts from his head and his blond mane. *Ponder later.*

He descended, and on the ground floor, he found a kitchen, a great hall, and a lesser hall beside it. Again, he saw no sign of men. Here, the mystery made his skull throb.

"It's all wrong," he whispered to himself. Perhaps if he spoke to himself, the conversation might bring to light what he was missing. And he felt reckless, eager to be done with his predicament. He searched the kitchen. While there was no sign of life, he did find a pantry. It was filled with grains, dried meat, cheese, and other sundries.

"The cannibals surely do not only eat the flesh of men," he said under his breath. "Why did these dainties go unspoiled? They never entered the keep. So..."

Brows furrowed, he headed into the main hall. Here was a long table for feasting, and at the end of the table two chairs, larger and more elaborate than the other, simpler furniture. He could hardly call them thrones, but they evoked the idea of royalty.

"More heads together are more likely to solve these conundrums," he said.

He turned to the main double doors and approached them. At once, he halted. A terrible thought struck him. The great doors were barred with a polished log of squared hardwood. *If all the men left the keep and the doors are barred from the inside...*

Skarde took a quick step toward the doors, intent on opening them post haste, but was frozen in an instant. Blasphemous shrieks filled the air. Never had he heard such hideous sounds – brittle, unearthly, piercing wails. He twirled about. His heart skipped a beat as a chill horror swept over him. Three black apparitions flew toward him from the door to the square tower, black cloaks fluttering behind them. Their heads – leering white skulls.

Skarde held his sword before him, his muscles tensing then releasing, ready for combat. A howling wraith swept on to the long table and sped down its length as the other two apparitions came down the aisle on either side. Their horrific keening increased, grieving his ears.

Reach out! Call upon my power or die, fool!

Mor's hot, crushing hand seemed to reach out for his mind. He retched at the defiling hold of Morsfangsel. The thought of relying on one black sorcery to counter another sent the cold fright of the supernatural down his spine – his soul was in jeopardy.

He had no time for fear. The wraith to his left swung a blade of earthly steel down at him. He leapt back as it nearly shaved the raised hair on his forearm. Skarde thrust his grey metal blade at the horror, its heft as quick as a bolt, but it pulled back just in time with a flutter of its shadowy cloak. He dashed the same way to avoid the attacks of the wraith leaping from the center and the right. One bounded over to the door, as if to block a path to it, and the other advanced with cautious thrusts. Skarde came back hard, but not deep and striking only at the thing's weapon. With an injured leg, his footwork left much to be desired. He knocked the weapon aside several times, but it spun the blade back with uncanny speed.

Suddenly, he broke away and ran toward the corner of the room. The wraith screamed with a ragged, ear-splitting wail and followed close. He spun to a halt and swung his blade high. The wraith swung to knock it aside, and Skarde brought his boot up and hard into its flanks. He connected with what felt like solid flesh.

"Unf!" the phantom grunted, and it fell to the floor.

He had no time for a killing stroke as the other two specters set upon him with whirling blades.

"Unf?" Skarde queried.

The two devils before him answered with more inhuman wails. He fought their savage strikes and wondered if ghosts tired. *If not, they will soon cut me to pieces*, he thought. To his dismay, the downed wraith had recovered and stood back up. Sprinting despite the pain, he circled the room and jumped upon a long side table. His long, muscle-banded legs carried him far ahead of his two pursuers, yet the third sought to cut him off before he could reach the main doors.

He hopped off the table and spun about. He grabbed a chair with his left hand, and continuing his turn, he hurled it at the wraith's skull-head as the thing hindered his path. The chair crashed into the devil's head, and its sword went clattering over the stones. It fell again, apparently stunned by the blow.

Skarde raised his sword high, and the blade quivered with anticipation for blood.

"Halt! You will not harm her!" a wraith behind him screamed.

The voice was stern but womanly. He did not expect such a plea from the undead, and so he stayed his blade. He glanced back, and the two creatures had frozen in place some ten paces behind him.

"Her?" Skarde said.

Weapon at the ready, he stepped wide around the sprawled figure and her weapon, and kept all three in his sight. Gazing down at the skull, he now saw a glint of eyes set deep in the sockets. The cranium was unnaturally large. The skull was a tight-fitting helm of split bone plates woven together.

"Take it off," he said.

The figure stared daggers at him. He gestured with his sword, indicating his willingness to continue the violence. Glancing back at the wraith that had commanded Skarde to stop, she received some unseen acquiescence. The figure gripped the skull face with a black-leathered hand and pulled the death's head off.

Thick dark hair spilled from the funereal façade to reveal a handsome woman with glittering dark eyes. Her brows knitted in a stern expression. Skarde regarded her with wide eyes. Then a hint of a smile cracked his otherwise severe face.

"Now you," Skarde said, gesturing Morsfangsel at them. "Toss your swords yonder and remove your masks."

The commanding wraith, taller than the others by a hand, gripped her skull and lifted it so slow as to be insolent. Skarde's eyes widened as a woman of incomparable beauty unveiled her face. Her defiant blue eyes held his, unwavering. Her chiselled features framed by a cascade of golden blonde hair. She glared at him in challenge.

Now he smiled broadly and gestured to the ground. "Aye, you'll have no more need of that steel, m'lady."

"By what right do you command me?" She said.

Skarde glanced at the two elaborate chairs at the end of the great table and back to her and laughed. "I'm the king of this castle now."

Her jaw clenched stiffly, and she held his gaze for a tense moment. She turned her eyes down at last and relented to his advantage. She tossed her sword over the table, and it clattered to the floor beyond. Having done so, the last wraith tossed the two swords it brandished as well, and pulled off its skull mask. Beneath was also a woman of great beauty, not so regal as her leader but with features familiar and sultry. Black hair tumbled over her shoulders and her mysterious eyes regarded him not with burning resentment, but with cool appraisal. For a moment, her eyes flickered over the naked thews of his legs and chest. Her magnificence was marred only by a wicked scar across her throat.

"There is a tale here!" Skarde said. "Come. You will tell it and plead your case among my men. Move slowly and stay before me."

"You fear three unarmed women, Palathorian dog?" The tall woman said.

"I know not who the Palathorians are, Lady. I am a pirate. A pirate with bad luck. And you are not unarmed. Warriors oft keep a second weapon on their person. This one before me has been curling her leg closer to her hand, inch by inch, as we speak. Does she have there an itch or a dagger?"

The woman before him cursed under her breath and cast him a venomous look as she straightened her leg. Skarde laughed.

"I feel there is a great misunderstanding between us. Let us parlay before we kill each other. I guess that you know many things about this place that I do not, and I... well, I have the upper hand by force."

Skarde did not wait for an answer but stepped back toward the doors. He did not take an eye off the women, who tensed like tigresses readying for a final battle. As he reached the doors and lay a hand on the bar, the tall woman raised her hand to halt. Skarde readied to leap forward to attack, but she shook her head, and the postures of the two other women slumped.

With a heave, Skarde tossed the bar to the ground and the keep's door creaked open, his men pushing at them. The dim light that filtered through the iron sky above hardly illuminated the room. Bardano stepped through and looked over the jumbled room, and the three beautiful women.

"Captain!" he said in surprise.

Chapter Ten

Skarde ushered the women out with a gesture. The blonde woman with aristocratic airs stepped toward her fallen companion and pulled her up by the forearm. Cupping her chin gently, she glanced into the shorter woman's eyes, and it seemed to him that some message passed between them.

"Are you injured, Klelia?" the tall woman whispered.

"Just bruises," she replied. "I can walk."

The tall woman held her tight for a moment and then glanced back at her other companion. The woman with the sultry eyes glided gracefully toward them, her black cloak fluttering over the stone. So smooth were her steps that Skarde thought she might be floating. She looked toward the tall woman and nodded. Together, the three followed Skarde's gesture into the courtyard. The men all stood with wide eyes upon the them, some with mouths open at their strangeness and beauty; others with hard stares for the misery they had inflicted.

Skarde noticed a small whitish object the size of a thumb on the ground where he had knocked the 'wraith' down. He picked it up and examined it as he exited the hall. It appeared to be made of bone... of what kind, he dared not guess. One end was carved in the fashion of a tiny skull, and on the other it was bored through. A guess as to what it was touched Skarde's mind. He held the end with the hole to his lips and blew into it. A wretched sound tore at the air with a hideous shriek. Men jumped at the note, and some pulled their swords. The captured women blanched as the men startled, fearing an attack... save for the tall woman who kept an aloof demeanor.

"A whistle!" Skarde laughed. "A whistle with a sound captured in the Nine Hells. I wonder why you have these, and your deathly disguises. But first, I would know who you are." He stared, eyes locked on the tall woman.

"You have no right to question the Baronetta!" Said Klelia. "You are trespassers on her estate!"

"Klelia!" The Baronetta said. "You say too much!"

Klelia clenched her jaw and cast her eyes down in vexation.

Skarde grinned. "Ho! Nobility! Quite a catch."

"I suppose you plan to ransom me," the Baronetta said.

"A fine idea, and one that would occur to me straight away in more usual hours. Right now, I bend my thoughts more to keeping my men out of the cannibals' gullets. In any case such a plan would yet be vulgar – I do not even know your name."

She held her head high, and Skarde saw her eyes twinkle with thought. "My name is Vajda, Baronetta of Dimitrou."

Skarde deemed her words as truth. *She is proud*, he thought. *A lie would be an admission of fear.* "And your companions?"

"Klelia of Pano," Vajda said, nodding at the sturdy form of the brown eyed woman. "The finest athlete in all of Saraylos." She turned and gestured at the sultry-eyed woman, "And this is Zlata."

He regarded her, and she returned his gaze, her eyes drizzling down his muscular form boldly. "Just Zlata? And forsooth why are you three here? I'd guess you make remarkable tales."

She regarded him with a mysterious mien.

"Well, have you nothing to say?" He said.

"She does not," Vajda said. "Her tongue has been cut out, and her throat slashed."

"Alas. But you three have some purpose other wise you would be dead with all the rest," Skarde said, nodding at Zlata. He turned back to their leader. "Vajda is not a Saraylosian name. Nor do they common bear blue eyes and hair of straw."

"No. I was born on the mainland to Count Vrasta of the Vanda people. I was raised within sight of the Savage Mountains."

"And almost as tall," Skarde said, eying her from foot to crown. "So, you were wed to a Saraylosian Baron…"

"Aye," Vajda interrupted. "Dull stuff. Marriages, accords, politics and such." She waved off further inquiry.

"Aye," Skarde agreed. "Tell me of your husband, your father, and your cousins later. I suspect you know much of these lands.

Speak, and we will devise a plan to escape them with our hides un-nibbled."

"My husband, as you might have guessed, is dead. Killed along with all the others whose remains you have taken upon yourselves to plunder and discard."

"May his spirit ride to Valhalla, or whatever God's hall his people revere," Skarde said.

"Valhalla is the place where warriors go, is it not? I have heard tales of the Northern people. No. He will not go there, wherever his spirit might fly. May he find peace."

Skarde raised his eyebrows at the widower's blithe mourning. Seeing Skarde's bafflement, she continued.

"He was a reluctant warrior," Vajda said. "True and brave in his own ways." Klelia rolled her eyes at this. "He was a man of Saraylos. Thinking of profits and gauging risks. He was no man of the frontier. It was I that persuaded him to build this castle, to seek wide lands for taming. To escape the stifling gardens and petty courts of Saraylos."

"Aye, I can grasp this need," Skarde said with a smile.

"Klelia gave me hope. She was born poor as a pauper, but by her own heart fixed upon a star, she grew in fame and glory."

"So, Baronetta, you, not your husband, are the warrior. You came here to escape the tedium of Saraylos."

Vajda eyes sharpened at this, and she seemed ready to retort at Skarde's framing. "Yes," she said, at length. "A crude way to put it, but close enough to the mark. Do not think that I merely hope to escape my duties. When we tame these lands, the Barony of Dimitrou will grow in power. We shall command a territory as large as Saraylos itself. We can entice thousands of farmers and herders to bolster our coffers. A new kingdom!"

"A worthy dream," Skarde said. "Alas for its passing. Let us now escape, and I swear I will leave you free to return to the courts of Saraylos."

Vajda laughed. "I will not return there. We shall stay here!"

Skarde all but choked on his next words. He noted that Klelia and Zlata gave each other a secretive and tense glance. "Stay?" he spat. "That is madness. You can not fend off the cannibals forever."

Vajda gave him a haughty look.

"These women," Grim-Face said, "by some spell or weirding have kept the cannibals away, even with the gates open."

"Ah... of course. So, you have frightened the savages off with cloaks, skulls, and whistles," Skarde said.

"Crudely put, again," the Baronetta said. "You guess the trappings but understand not the reasons. I traveled among the savages when they were not so hostile, before the coming of that wicked shaman. When they defeat enemies, they consume their flesh, and thereby their spirits. They gain the powers of their enemies, and some portion of their soul. No one of them will consume a whole individual, for fear that they will lose themselves. Even when the whole tribe partakes, there are parts of the devoured that remain. These, last shreds, are not just body, but also soul. Chamobodg, the God of death, winter and misfortune comes for these unfortunates. On a black wind, he rides, a naked skull, tortured souls howling at his approach! He, alone, keeps the tattered souls of the consumed from seeking terrible vengeance, but he is feared above all."

Skarde shook his head. "The Gods are subtle, unlike their priests. I would not place bets on the comings and goings of Gods. They have higher things to attend, save on rare occasions. Yet, to parody such an ill-starred deity seems ill-considered. I see no good end to this, woman. Come away from this terrible place. Use these wraith-like disguises once more to spook the savages. Less than one day would we need to repair our ship, now floundered on the shore. We will be away and free of this land's curses!"

"We will stay," Vajda said. "The house of Dimitrou will not abandon this place and this opportunity. They will come to reinforce us!"

Skarde cursed her stubbornness. "Don't be a fool! How long has it been since you have seen hide or hair of your late husband's house?"

Her face stiffened in a mask of loathing. She stared at him with eyes that could cut flesh. At once, he lamented his sharp tongue, but offered no apology.

"Maybe, my Lady," Klelia said stepping forward, "the savage's tongue is vulgar, but speaks true?" Klelia turned to Skarde with a hint of anger in her eyes. "Every month, a small ship came and brought news and supplies. We have not seen anyone since the cannibals attacked."

"Klelia! You do not know mercenary men. They are without honor. They will get what they want from us and then use us. And when they are done pleasuring themselves, they are as like as not to murder us or sell us into slavery."

Skarde couldn't deny that his men had cast a longing eye at the women, even though they had killed some of their companions. He had, himself, regarded the three beauties with appreciation. "You need not fear while I live, Baronetta. By my word, you will not be ravished or assaulted."

"What contract would hold you to such a promise?" Vajda said. "You are lawless men."

Skarde's face darkened. "To Hell with the signing of some scrap of paper. Lawless, I am, and a savage. It is the civilized man that act without honor unless some greater power holds them to account. I speak an oath! My word is honor. My word is a bond made of sterner stuff than the blathering treaties of the civilized."

"Captain!" Came a sudden shout from the parapets. "Come right away… disaster!"

Skarde looked up. The few archers that remained on the wall to watch for any movement of the enemy were distracted by the drama unfolding in the courtyard. Now, they all looked westwards with wide eyes and gaping mouths. Skarde bolted to the northern stairs and flew up them. Close behind came

Grim-Face, Savo, and the Baronetta, uninvited yet bold. The archers all pointed at the shore in dismay. Desperate hate welled up in Skarde's heart and he clenched his jaw and fist in fury. Where the mast of the ship had jutted like a thin needle above the trees, now a billowing cloud of smoke curled into the sky, its lower portions glowing red.

"Damn you to the Nine Hells!" Skarde shouted at the trees.

He saw no movement or figure, but a din arose of jeering and cruel laughter, muffled by distance and the trees. The tendrils of white smoke gathered into a pale column over the sea. The courtyard fell silent, and the faces of the men grew ashen as they realized what was happening. The jabbering of the horde in the forest echoed and reverberated – a steady drone accompanied by a slow wavering pitch reaching higher and higher. Some chant lifted from the eerie song, and it became clear and menacing.

"Look," Belgeti said, pointing away far left of smoke of the burning ship.

Their heads turned and from the forest came a man, arms outstretched under the antlers of a magnificent buck skull. His body, beneath a great cloak of dark furs and shoulder blade bone spaulders, was decorated with smeared black paint in the fashion of his fellows. His long, white beard marked him as an elder, but his sinews appeared hale.

"Og-Riz," the Baronetta swore under her breath.

He let out a piercing cry, as if to mock the death-whistles they used. The chants of the cannibals hidden under the boughs behind him seemed to emanate from his direction. He mouthed those incomprehensible words. Shouting and raising his hands towards the sky like claws, his words flowed, almost slurred before strafing out in sharp edges.

"Og-Riz?" Skarde said to Vajda. "Be this the shaman you spoke of?"

"Og-Riz is their word for shaman. It is he of whom I spoke. His name is Kampu."

"You know their language?" Skarde asked with raised eyebrows. "What does he say?"

"I know only a few words. He riles his tribesmen. He has named us sworn enemies and is now saying something like: *Interlopers, you awaken the spirit of death. A winter will come early. Freeze you, Starve you. Peirce you with spears and cold.* He waxes poetic. I'm sure he is having the desired effect upon his kinsmen."

"Ho! Old man!" Skarde yelled. "Quit your yammering! It's too early in the morning! Go take a bath!"

The shaman spat back some savage curse, and Vajda rolled her eyes at both of them.

"Shall we shoot him?" Belgeti said. "He's within bowshot."

"Only just..." Skarde began.

"No!" Vajda said. "You would set the cannibals' passions afire. We won't hold them off long if their fear of their deathly spirits is overcome. Come! Let us not bicker before his eyes."

The Baronetta stormed down the steps, followed by a few of the men. Skarde turned and regarded those men with burning eyes. She looked back and caught his gaze.

"Do you think yourself lord of the castle?" Skarde said.

"Do you?" She barked, looking up at him with a cold glare. "Bravado and brash is all I have seen from you. Would you not negotiate with him, even if only to trick him?"

Skarde eyed the shaman, still shouting curses at him. He walked to the stairs, speaking as he descended. "If he wanted us to leave, he could have given us passage to our boat. Perhaps it is *you* that has offended him. Perhaps, he angles for greater sway over the many clans that have been brought together. Holy men often gather power under such banners."

"You sacrilege the gods..." she began.

"Not the gods, just their priests," Skarde said. "Too many are tricksters and as worldly as any noble."

She hissed air through her teeth in anger at the jab. "You could have made better use of the exchange, nonetheless. What leader are you if you do not improve our circumstances?"

A low murmur rose among the men.

Skarde tugged his beard in thought and frustration. "We will not leave. Not unless I can think of something. Our ship is destroyed! Do you still believe you will lord over reinforcements?"

"My hopes were greater before you came..."

"Hopes maybe, but what of proofs?" Skarde said. "Did reinforcements arrive, only to be slain? Does Dimitrou dare send a significant portion of its strength with your rivals... the Palathori? Do they cause Dimitrou trouble even now?"

"The Palathori," Vajda said between clenched lips.

"Do they hinder your house? Does the new Baron of Dimitrou even wish for your return?" Skarde wagged his finger at her. "You seem the troublesome type."

Vajda's face darkened and she turned from him to pace the courtyard. Klelia looked upon Skarde with a furled brow and tight lips, but Zlata had watched the exchange closely with a fanciful and distant expression. Skarde turned to her and caught her eye.

"We will die if we stay. Even if our food were to last, would you stay a prisoner here until winter brought death?" Skarde asked of her.

Her eyes widened quizzically as if she were amused, and she glanced at the Baronetta. Vajda spun about.

"And you would lead us to freedom? You led your pirates into this quandary after who know what fool's judgement. Is it not so?"

Skarde shrugged. "No more foolish than in any dangerous venture. I could say the same about you."

"If you think..." Vajda began, almost shouting.

"Cease!" Grim-Face shouted. "The both of you, enough! One way or another, we must leave. My lady, would you please help us to understand what happened here? How did it come to pass that the whole garrison was slain, and the drawbridge left open?"

The Baronetta looked about at the seventy pairs of eyes fixed upon her and took a deep breath, as if gathering her thoughts. "I will explain what I can, though it was a strange night. We have several villages beyond the cleft in the mountains. From the beach to cliff, there is good game to be found, but the ground is rough and unsuitable for farming. Beyond the range there are plains. After some clearing, they made for excellent farmlands. The cannibals gave us only a little trouble. The villages were settled by retired soldiery and could well handle themselves. Any greater threats were put down by our garrison.

Trouble came when we began clearing a path through the thickets of the cleft in the mountains. We had only a rocky trail clinging to the southern slope – wholly unsuitable for wagons. We needed a good road for our villagers, as taking goods upon one's own back, or with a lone horse would no longer suffice. We endeavor to cut a way through the forest there. It seems it is a holy place to them. That is when the attacks came. Soon after, that insidious Og-Riz appeared."

"Aha!" Skarde said. "It seems to me that this is where some negotiation could have taken place, that or decisive action."

Vajda regarded him cold, hard eyes, but Grim-Face stood between the two.

"Go on, Lady Vajda," Grim-Face spoke in a soothing tone so unlike his visage.

Skarde's lips tightened, and he paced the courtyard, though he kept his ears on the Baronetta's words.

"Our garrison, then, was engaged in patrolling the cleft. In addition to these, we employed many scouts and foresters. Most trusted among these was young Cyriacos. He oft would report to Kudres, my husband, after he returned from the field. I paid little mind 'til he spoke of a field of black stones, pillars shaped like skulls where ancient spirits dwell. He left without being dismissed. He seemed to be in a fey mood."

"No doubt he is that one in the winch house!" Skarde interrupted. "He murdered a guard."

"If you know the tale better than I, continue," she said.

"We are over eager," Grim-Face said. "I beg, continue."

"The cannibals were already in the courtyard as we saw ourselves. We got word that he went mad, murdered the winch guard, cut the bridge ropes to open the gate, and slit his own throat. The few men that were in the keep made a sortie, and I with them. Klelia and Zlata came with me, but it was hopeless. There were hundreds of the savages and too many of the garrison slaughtered before a defence could be mounted. I led my companions back to the keep with little hope. But Zlata had some cunning prepared."

She nodded at Zlata, who smiled at the compliment and acknowledgment.

"She had fashioned skull helms and death-whistles to go along with black cloaks we had. So, we dressed as the dread servants of Chamobodg, come to collect souls. I thought it a desperate ploy, sure to end in our deaths. What choice did we have? We emerged from the tunnel door, and the cannibals fled. They are a superstitious lot and would not interfere with or approach us in that guise."

"Magnificent," Skarde said, smiling at Zlata.

She returned the compliment with a nod and the scantest hint of a smile. Skarde looked at Vajda, who refused to meet his gaze, and then turned to look at the cloud of smoke from their ship, now grown huge and ominous and visible over the walls from the court.

"Take the men inside and feed them," Skarde said to Belgeti, Bardano, and Grim-Face. "Scour every last inch of the castle for anything useful. Take the women as well. Beware, our guests are no doubt still armed."

"As I thought," Vajda spat.

"And let no harm come to them. No man shall lay a lusty hand on them. That is my word. I will go and consider our next move."

Vajda complained no more, as Bardano followed Skarde's command, but she had defiance in her eye. Klelia kept by her mistress' side, and Zlata took a moment to gaze at Skarde as he mounted the stairs to the wall. He stared out over the sea of tree tops at the smoke. No plan came to him, but a deep melancholy. After long minutes of brooding, a man climbed the stairs. Belgeti stood beside him.

"I was a boy of meager means among the fisherfolk of the mountains and seas of the North. Do you believe in fate?" Skarde said.

"You are in a philosophical mood?"

"Ha! I but wonder if the weavers of fate I have flouted are laughing in revenge. There goes our treasure. It burns and will wash away with the ashes into the sea. A comfort it would be for the rest of our lives, but also a greater thing – power. To take hold of the threads of fate and weave them as we would."

"Do we not already have that? Still, I said I would not return to my home without glory," Belgeti said. "If I defy a fate set for me, why did the gods put this hunger in my heart. This is a setback. Perhaps a test. Who knows what the gods play at? I can only be certain that I yearn to try some cured meats, if they have some."

"Then let us eat now," Skarde said. "We have much to discuss. Tomorrow we will do whatever need calls for."

Chapter Eleven

Skarde paced the parapets as the sun, a grey glow hidden behind grey clouds, sank into the sky. His temples throbbed. He stopped to gaze out at the forest. He stood for a long while letting his eyes trace paths between the trees. *I can hardly think. If only I could run through the trees until I was exhausted. There is little to think about. We must go.* He looked down at his men, languishing in the courtyard. The keep was open to them, but few chose to enter it. *We must go. I will not fail them, but great danger awaits us. We must dare it.*

Skarde descended the stairs and called for his chief men. He strode into the keep, sat at the great table, and picked a sliver of dried meat that had been set upon it, and chewed. He grabbed a wineskin that had been found among the keep stores, leaned back in the chair and threw his booted feet upon the table. Looking down the table, he raised the skin to the Baronetta who had seated herself in one of the high-back chairs. Klelia sat in the other. He took a swig, and she shot him a dire look. *I may die tomorrow, but I shall enjoy this moment.* The men came in, eager to hear the plans they assumed he had conjured up. He let the men settle in, and they all stared at him waiting.

"Well, captain?" Savo said, breaking the waiting silence.

"Well," said Skarde. "Well, well, well, well, well."

"The plan?" He asked.

"Aye," said Skarde. "I have thought on it long, and there is little to think on. I only see one path forward, and few strategies or trickeries to assure our success. Our best hope is to make for the villages on the other side of the cleft..."

"The Vodionatar, we call it," Vajda said in a corrective tone.

Skarde smiled and nodded. "The Vodionatar, then... we go through to the other side."

"We must fight the whole lot then," Grim-Face said.

"Aye, but I said we had few tricks, not none. I will take Hochnay and Belgeti over the walls before the glow of dawn comes and we will head into the forest where the road passes in. There, we will don the wraith disguises and frighten the cannibals off."

Right away, a clamor began, and men began shouting in surprise and dismay. The Baronetta leaned forward, uttering curses.

"Let me go!" Bardano said, leaning forward. "For Ilkar!"

"Madness!" said Savo and Tarsazi at the same time.

"I will not let you steal our only means of defense," the Baronetta said when the clamour died down.

"I didn't ask," Skarde said.

She laughed with a sneer. "As I thought. You renege on your word. You are a thief."

Skarde's eyes twinkled over a wry smile. "I gave you my word, and I mean to keep it. You and your charges will not be ravished or harmed. As for theft... I am a pirate."

"You will leave us defenseless. We will be harmed," she sneered.

"I had hoped you would change your mind and come with us. You can fight, and swords would be welcome, for surely, there will be as much fighting as we can handle. As for your defense, it will not keep you through winter. And how much longer do you think the brutes will remain fooled?"

"I wonder that, too," Belgeti said, nodding at Savo and Tarsazi.

"You will not come?" Skarde said.

The Baronetta gave him a hard stare, and Skarde thought he spotted reluctant acquiescence in her eyes.

"It will be dangerous. I wonder if the old shaman will scare so easy," Belgeti said. "He seems crafty. Still, I will go."

"He is crafty, and I doubt he will be fooled," Skarde said. "Yet the tribesmen were. He can not so easily dismiss the wraiths of Chamobodg, I'd guess, without diminishing his own mystic authority. He must deal with us as if we were true spirits."

"Aye," Belgeti said, tugging at his wispy beard. "Yet whatever he conjures up will not be long waiting."

"Not long," Skarde said. "I only hope for enough time for the rest of us to escape the castle. Perhaps we can get some lead on them, and then we run or ambush them as chance allows."

"Captain, I beg you, let me go," Bardano said.

The Baronetta stood and spoke over all with a commanding voice. "I will go, and Klelia and Zlata will join me."

"You are a fool and likely to get us all killed," she said. "I would have this done a-right. I know the paths of the forest. I know the savages better than thee. I will drive them off and join you in the Vodionatar. That is a strange place and can be disorienting. Keep the south face of the cleft mountain to your right and stay together. When we reach the closest village, you may go on your way, and we will return to the castle."

"If the villages remain," Skarde said.

"I have no doubt," Vajda said. "They are walled, and the people are armed and able."

"So be it!" Skarde said, keeping his skepticism to himself. "By paths foul or fair our way lies thus. Rest as you can, men, until the small hours."

The pervading air of doom did not lift during the night, and the men slept fitfully, expecting battle and death against a foe many times their number. But as the hour approached, at least, there came the vigor of momentum, and a desire to come to grips with their enemy. None had to be roused as Skarde and

Grim-Face prepared the grappling lines on the west side of the castle walls near the cliff face.

Vajda entered the courtyard and every man's face turned toward her, Klelia and Zlata following close. They wore their black wraith cloaks and their swords strapped to their backs. Zlata carried a sack of grey cloth, and in it were their skull helms and death-whistles. They climbed the stairs and met the gigantic Northman upon the wall.

"Are you prepared?" he said to her in his strange accent.

"I am always prepared," she said.

"May Thunir's might go with you," he said.

A rebuke of the barbarian's god was upon her lips, but she held it back. *No. Harsh words with an ally, even a fleeting ally, is bad luck before battle.* "What kind of god is he?" She asked, instead.

"He is strong and comes at the head of a storm. Warriors look to him in battle," said the Northman.

"We look to Tharun. He is the king of the Gods, he strikes with lightning, a golden axe to cleave foes in battle, and rules with wisdom in peace. Guide your men with his boon," she said.

Skarde nodded and patted the crenel upon which the hook and rope had been secured. Lowering the gate was a noisy affair, so they climbed. She hopped atop it and swung her legs over the side. Taking hold of the rope, she stole down the wall, a shadow in the gloom. Klelia followed and spoke no word to the giant of a man. Vajda embraced her as she lit upon the stone ground at the base of the wall.

"We will return, Klelia dear, and with fewer flesh eaters, and no pirates to contend with," she said.

"I begrudge that they stay within our walls, while we are expelled," Klelia said.

"We sally, not run," Vajda said.

Looking up, she saw Zlata attending to some words spoken by the Northman. She made some sign, and they clasped hands before she climbed down to take hold of the rope. She landed, and Vajda caught her eye in the dark.

"You make some pact with the barbarian?" Vajda said.

Zlata nodded and made a sign.

"He is our ally... this hour, but what of the next?"

Zlata made a series of signs with agitated hands.

"A blessing? Or a concord?"

Zlata sighed and said nothing, looking out over the cliff face to the forest far beneath.

"So, you agree with him, do you not?" Vajda said.

Zlata opened the bag slung over her shoulder and plucked out a skull, handing it to Vajda. As Vajda took it, Zlata made a sign of peace.

Vajda shook her head and sighed. "I do not expect treachery from you, *Tzaera of Blades*... we will debate later."

The three crept low to the ravine and came almost to the swift moving waters. Vajda glanced back at the others. The roar of the falls, muted by tall outcroppings of stone, now roared and its cool spray could be felt. So close were they to the falls that if they fell and were swept away, they would have little chance. Here, even the moonlight did not reach, and they crawled along by feel and memory. It seemed a long, slow haul to the edge of the forest, but at last, they arrived.

"We've made it, unseen," Vajda said, counting on the roar of the river to cover her voice. "You two go east and scare the savages in the forest. I will go north. I expect Kampu will camp on easier ground there. I will frighten them as deep into the trees as I might. Maybe slay him..."

"Don't," Klelia said, her eyes wide. "It is too dangerous. He will be protected. By men – and perhaps by spirits."

"Don't worry," Vajda said, reaching out to smooth her hair. "I will not so easily be driven into the Pits. I would send a hundred before me."

Klelia's face hardened, not liking Vajda's answer. Zlata produced a skull helm and handed it to Klelia. She slipped it over her unhappy face and took a whistle as well. In moments, the three were ready. The Baronetta gave a signal. Klelia and Zlata danced over stones to the other side of the ravine toward the road. Vajda turned and climbed the northern bank.

Into the trees, she dove. Now unconcerned with stealth, she kept an eye sharp for natural snares and savages. Shrill, soul chilling shrieks sounded in the distance. Her companion wraiths had found victims. *Where are mine?* She wondered.

Now, on the left, she spotted a savage coming to investigate. She sounded her whistle and he let out a gurgling cry of fear before bounding away. She gave chase. He was swift and flew before her, screaming out in terror. Only a handful of figures fled in the darkness before her, where she had expected them to leap away like a wave of frightened grasshoppers.

For minutes, she pursued him, and at last, she slowed, suspecting an ambush or a trick. *Those damn pirates should be on their way down the road. Do the savages plan an ambush there?* She halted and listened. There was no sound of battle. She kept on, right around the clearing through the forest to the cliff face had she gone. No other cannibals had she found.

"They have all moved into The Vodionatar for an ambush!" Vajda spoke to herself aloud.

How could they know our plans? Vajda thought as she ran back. The towering Northman was arrogant and uncouth, but seemed true to his word, and the other pirates were less villainous than she had expected. She did not want them in her castle, but neither did she desire a grim death for them. *Does Kampu see and hear over our walls? Does he cast bones? Or does he simply guess well? Whatever his gambit, I must warn them.*

Vajda heard the faint call of the death-whistles in the distance. She ran through the forest, traversed the river, and crossed the road in haste. She tracked her compatriot's shrieks, and when close, she gave three sharp blows on her whistle. They called back, and after a few minutes, they had found each other again.

The sky peeking through the branches above glowed an orange devoid of warmth.

"Lady!" Klelia called out, and grasped Vajda tightly about her waist. "You live! Did you slay the Og-Riz?"

"Nay," Vajda said, holding Klelia tight. "I hardly came across any savages.

"We chased some number. It is hard to count them in the dark – fifty, perhaps."

"I fear Kampu has scried our plans," Vajda said. "Come, let us trail the pirates and warn them."

"You would rescue the brutes?" Klelia said.

Zlata grabbed Klelia by the shoulder and nodded.

"I understand, Klelia," Vajda said. "But it seems ignoble to let them fly to their deaths unwarned when they have been as true to their words as pirates might be. And besides, if they must fight, I would rather have the pirates win, or at the least, inflict terrible losses to the cannibals."

"Lady. It's just... the way he spoke to you in your very hall..."

"Aye, it made my blood boil. But he is a captain in his own right, if a fool. I would guess he fought his way up from a lowly station. Not unlike yourself."

"Lady, I beg you, do not compare me to him!"

Zlata blew her death-whistle and interrupted their argument. Already moving, she waved them forward.

Skarde and Hochnay gripped the spoked handles of the winch. It seemed unduly long since the women went over the walls. They'd had enough time to enacted their plan.

"Nine Hells, those pig-headed wenches had best not gotten themselves killed," Skarde said.

Hochnay laughed, and spoke in a thick accent, "Ye've let them get under yer skin."

"Aye. Nettles do that," Skarde said.

"Och, aye. But I do fancy the tall one. She's nearly yer height but far better fer the looking."

"She does have her charms. Yet, I don't think she would say the same of you," Skarde said.

"Aye, but one'a them surely must fancy my red locks."

Skarde laughed. "Wait... do you hear?"

In the distance, they heard the horrid wailing of the death-whistles. Coming from a distance through a dark, menacing forest did not diminish its power to send chills up his spine. He signaled to Hochnay and the two twirled the winch as fast as they could. The drawbridge plummeted and thudded on the stones on the other side of the stream. With so many men, there was little hope in stealth. Grim-Face and Bardano led the first of the men across the wooden platform. The young man was proud to be picked as a leader of the vanguard.

Hochnay flew from the winch room, and Skarde followed close behind him down the stairs. They joined Belgeti and the archers in the rear of the column, in case the archers were attacked. The formation sprinted, quick and silent along the road, and then through the jumble of tree stumps. Skarde's bandaged leg burned as he jogged, but he kept pace with a stiff upper lip. In a long minute, they reached the forest edge, and they heard again the shrill cries of the whistles to either side. No sight of cannibals did they catch. Skarde drew his sword slung across his back. It sent a tingle through his hand.

The whole column slowed under the trees. They could not sprint for hours, and the reasonable pace allowed them to better watch for attack. After ten minutes of running, Skarde shook his head in disquiet and turned to Hochnay.

"Something is amiss," Skarde said. "I expected our foe to attack by now, or at least to toss a few javelins at us from the trees and flee. Nothing!"

"Aye. I've a peely-weely feeling in mah guts."

"You are keen and woodcrafty. Hang back in the bush for a few minutes, and follow us." Skarde pointed up the huge foothill towards the cleft. "We will meet you atop the slope just before the mountain splits. If they are coming up behind us in force, catch up and warn us!"

"Aye," Hochnay nodded, and he turned to dive into the shadowed trees.

Skarde continued along, ignoring the burning in his leg. He sped to catch the front of the column. There, he found Bardano and Grim-Face. His ugly lieutenant eyed him, and Skarde could see his concern in the dim but growing light.

"I've sent Hochnay back a bit to keep a watch behind us," Skarde said.

Grim-Face seemed relieved. "Wise."

Skarde ran beside them for a while, his mind distracted with thoughts of how Grim-Face had saved the situation between he and the Baronetta. "Shrewd in some matters, in others..." Skarde struggled to speak. "My tongue is often sharp..."

"Aye, it is captain," he said.

"Do you speak of your words with Vajda?" Bardano said. "She is unreasonable! You owe her no apology."

"Maybe she is, maybe she isn't," Grim-Face said. "What matters that to us? We needed a concord and every ally we can muster."

"Still, she should apologize, not the captain," Bardano said.

"Apologize?" Skarde laughed. "No, that she-devil will offer me none. But I do offer thanks to Grim-Face for his quick thinking, and soothing words."

Grim face nodded in acceptance and kept running.

After an hour along the waning trail, they at last came to the cleft. The road, now just a scrub covered trail, topped the foothill and led toward a stream – one of many that was fed by quick creeks and waterfalls from the split peaks. The mountains loomed over them. The western face rose quick, but trees clung to it, their numbers dwindling near the summits. As they entered, the southern face of the closest rise on their right was sheer, as if a god had cut the stone with an axe the size of the moon. A sinister looking forest of dark pine, beech, oak, and poplar welcomed them between the vice of the mountain faces.

Skarde called a halt and looked about. The Vodionatar rose some mile or so before them, but they could see behind them westwards clear over the trees for miles from their high vantage.

"Let us wait here, briefly mind you, for Hochnay and whatever news he brings," Skarde said.

Belgeti came running forward and joined Savo and Grim-Face at Skarde's side.

"Too easy," Belgeti said, eyeing the pass with suspicion. "Do you think they will ambush us in there?"

Skarde sniffed at the air as if he could smell an answer. Some warning itched his uncivilized instinct, but no premonition came to him. The light, the air, even the feel of the grit under his boots seemed off, as if it, or he, were out of time and place. He shook his head and focused on the task at hand. "Maybe. That, or they will come from behind at some opportune spot. I did not expect to escape without a scratch."

They waited, almost seventy of them, in total silence, listening to the whispers in the wind. The sun peaked out from behind thick clouds and caressed their backs with warmth.

"I do not like sitting on this bare hilltop, the sun shining a lantern beam upon us," Savo said.

"No," Skarde said. "I also like it not. Hochnay has had time thrice over to catch us up. Where is he? Let us move forward at a cautious pace. If he lives, he will find us. Come! Be wary to the fore, the back, and to either side."

Skarde surveyed the land, drinking in every detail before he led them down a gentle slope that turned upward again, following a nearby stream. He sent two men forward, and two men back to scout, hoping against his instincts that trouble would not find them. The trees began to huddle about them, and as the nearby undergrowth thickened, the air itself smelled old. It led them to a rising path of scree and stone wide enough for four or five men to walk abreast.

"To the Hells with this place. My gut tells me we should move," Skarde said.

None argued, and they marched on. Finding the stony high path was not difficult, and they set their feet upon it with trepidation in their hearts. The stone faces of the Vodionatar, a rough mile apart, seemed ready to come together like the hands of a titan and crush them. Light from the morning sun glowed dim as a blanket of heavy grey clouds rolled over them. The sky darkened as they entered the shadows of the pass. It became cooler, clouds loomed, and mists slithered down the bony rock fingers of the cliffs east and west.

"Captain!" boomed a voice from behind, loud enough to set Skarde's teeth on edge.

"Quiet fool!" he growled as one of the scouts he had sent behind came sprinting up the path.

"Apologies! Captain, Hochnay and the wraith-women approach. They bear dire warnings!"

Skarde's head wheeled about as he tried to bend his eyes around a rocky turn. He half expected an army of cannibals to charge about it, or appear from under the boughs of the forest below them. He waved a halt to all and ran with Belgeti and a few others back the way they had come. His naked blade flung dew as he ran. The mists crawling up the scrabble embankment to the path obscured the way behind.

He spotted the tousled red beast of Hochnay's hair, and beside him ran the Amazonian form of the Baronetta. Close behind them were Klelia and Zlata. Hochnay waved his sword high, almost as if he were charging into battle. Skarde halted and waited for his approach.

"Captain!" Hochnay said, his chest pumping for air. "A trap!"

Vajda breathed deep. "I knew this plan of yours was too simple," she said, pausing for another inhalation. "The old wolf has not been fooled! We are in mortal peril!"

"Out with it, woman! What peril!" Skarde growled, as much angered by the jab as by the wasting of breath on it.

"Zlata, Klelia, and I frightened off a few of the savages, but far too few. Kampu himself is nowhere to be seen."

"The old wolf is sly," Skarde said. "I thought our escape too easy. So... he lies before us."

"Before us, behind us... or he brews some other trouble.," Vajda said.

"Is there a place we could ambush them?" Skarde asked.

"In the Vodionatar, I know not. It is a strange place and I have only traveled the path we are on. Of the forest paths, I know little."

"We must turn back," Klelia said.

The Baronetta looked far off, her noble face a mask for her churning thoughts. "Now that Kampu has us out of our shell, he will not allow us to return so easily."

Chapter Twelve

"The Old Wolf is the headwaters from which a river of troubles flow," Skarde growled through clenched teeth. "When the body of the pack is relieved of its head, it falls into chaos," Skarde said. He took a step toward the steep hill of rubble and rugged trees that formed the slope between the forest below and the path.

Vajda laughed. "You can't be serious. Will you wander through the forest blind until Kampu throws himself on your sword?"

"You offer no better plan," Skarde said.

"I'll go with you," Bardano said.

Skarde regarded him with approval but shook his head. "I'll need your sword arm here with Grim-Face, Tarsazi, and Farasid. It is almost certain you will face a fight. I will not succeed with a host. I will be the ghost in the fog this time."

"Surely, you can't go alone," Bardano said.

"I will go," Vajda said.

Now a crowd formed about them. Klelia came to the Baronetta's side, a miserable look on her face, and Zlata with her.

"Will you wander blind with me?" Skarde said sharply.

"No. I know where Kampu may be, though it is only a chance. The Great Skull Totem. I have not been there, but I have spoken to scouts who have."

"No," Klelia said.

Vajda gripped Klelia by her shoulders and stared into her eyes tenderly. "Fear not. I will be back before nightfall. Zlata – guide them."

Zlata nodded as Skarde shot Grim-Face a warning glance. He also nodded.

"Skarde, will ye not take another?" Hochnay asked.

"Aye, if a small group of us go, you should be among them. Belgeti, you and your two best archers, Ramzi and Oğuz, should come also."

"Ah, a chance at a glorious death, chu-chu-chu," he laughed.

Six figures crept under dark boughs that loomed over them like giant grasping hands. Though mist wrapped them in a blanket of secrecy, they moved slow and silent, hardly rustling the forest detritus under their feet. Vajda, weapon drawn like the rest, led them, and every two score paces they halted to watch and listen for the slightest woodland noise out of place.

It was during one of these brief halts that Belgeti took notice of the trees. Here the familiar fir, birch, and ash common in the lower forest took on an outlandish seeming. Thicker, darker... and grim. Dank mosses lay underfoot, and alien looking fungus climbed the trunks. He intuited that in the days of the ancestors of his people these trees were already old. Ducking under a low hanging limb, gnarled branches scraped at his back. He shuddered at the ghoulish touch.

Although they moved in a tangled line, Vajda did not lead them through any impenetrable foliage or difficult ravines. Foot by twisted foot they made their way toward what seemed the center of the cleft.

"I feel as if a thousand eyes are on me," Belgeti whispered to Skarde.

"Aye. This is the enemy's haunt, and we near the heart of their devilry. I smell great danger here. I wish I had come alone."

Vajda turned to stare daggers at them and let out a low hiss for silence. "I wish many things, but for now stay alert. The Og-Riz prepares some black magic... can you not feel it in the air."

"There is nought that is right here. I would not notice one more devil," Skarde said.

Skarde ushered Vajda forward, and she shot him an imperious glower before moving on. Belgeti waved his men on behind him. On they went, but they had not topped the next rise before Hochnay dropped to his haunches. Skarde followed him in half a heartbeat, and the rest a moment after that. His mop of red hair shook as he looked this way and that. Belgeti saw nothing, but quietly knocked an arrow.

Then, like a bolt, Hochnay charged toward a grey turret of stones just off the course they had been following. Skarde followed just as quick, and by their own wood-magic neither made more than a rustle. Painted cannibals slithered from their hiding holes to meet the onrushing Northmen. The Baronetta, taken aback for a blink of an eye at their sudden action now sped into the fray.

Belgeti gasped. He pulled his bow, took aim, and let fly in one smooth well practiced movement. Twenty savages at least surrounded the three melee combatants, but now one stumbled as an arrow sprouted from his chest. His men took aim, but the melee sprawled into a chaotic swarm of bodies, and they could not chance striking one of their own. Hochnay held three at bay as much by swinging his mighty sword as by his maniacal screams. Skarde pressed forward with an oath, seemingly heedless of the savage's flint tipped spears. He slew one, then another before the brutes threw themselves away from him.

Seeing the whirlwind of death the two titanic Northmen brewed, the remaining cannibals surrounded Vajda. She danced among their deadly stalks, batted them away, and with lightning strokes pierced two to match Skarde. But they encircled her like jackals.

"Swords fly!" Belgeti shouted. He drew his blade, urged his two men on, and raced toward the overwhelmed woman. It was too late. Belgeti was too far away as a painted foe lunged at her unprotected back. The foe raised his spear to drive it into her spine.

Then like a bolt, a grey metal sword flew through the air and pierced him between his shoulder blades. He froze, the ghastly look of death in his eyes. Skarde had seen the ambush, and pounced through the air, throwing his sword to meet the enemy one heartbeat sooner, and just in time. He landed like a great hunting cat behind the dead man before he had time to slump to the ground, pulled the sword from its sheath of flesh and bone, and whirled in a red arc to slay another.

Vajda spun and brought her sword down hard at Skarde's back, only to smash away a spear tip a hand's breadth from his flesh. She leapt forward and skewered the offender before kicking, with all the strength of a man, another savage who had gotten too close.

Now Belgeti, Ramzi, and Oğuz joined the melee. Several more cannibals fell before the companion's onslaught. Though still almost thrice their number, the savages retreated. It was no rout, and they simply gave way before any threat of a sword blow. They pursued.

They heard a sizzling sound and saw a smoky glow through the trees. Belgeti blinked his eyes, wondering if they might be deceived. Coming over the rise sped four cannibal warriors carrying blazing brands as long as spears and topped with ash-blackened human skulls. Below the skulls were tied bunches of outlandish looking dark green leaves. These hissed, burned, and billowed thick grey smoke.

The stave wielding cannibals set upon their flanks. The smoke bearers wailed with pandemoniac shrieks thrusted their devilish crosiers at the six defenders. Belgeti choked at the acrid vapours and struck out with his sword at the closest. The savage darted back and violently shook his haft, sending a fresh wave of smoke at them. A tinge of fear gripped his guts as he realized that the cannibals stood down breeze and avoided the fumes.

Belgeti felt his throat tighten. The foe seemed both far away and close enough to slash at. They became drab silhouettes in mockery of human form from which colors wept away and dribbled to the ground. They were about him, but his sword was useless. A blunt pain seized Belgeti's head, and he knew darkness.

Bardano's eyes narrowed and his jaw tightened as the sword-witch, Zlata, fell into place beside Grim-Face and Tarsazi. The two men spoke, but Bardano could not catch the conversation over the constant scrabbling of stones under so many boots. Zlata made signs with her hands, but he only half caught them, and her expressive face was turned away from him. Eyeboga, who had fallen back to keep an eye on what paths Skarde and company took, now caught up with him.

"I do not trust her, my friend," Bardano said. "She might lead us to a trap."

"I do not trust her either," Eyeboga said, "but she is no friend to the savages. I worry more about this Klelia. She seems entirely devoted to her mistress. The silent one at least seems to question."

"She's all the more dangerous, then."

Eyeboga's lip turned up in lukewarm agreement. "Just keep your eyes open."

Bardano shook his head. His eyes darted from side to side and his palms sweated as they passed every turn and jutting crag. The idea that they could better hold off an enemy on a narrow path crumbled if they passed blind corners and places where ambushes could easily be set.

"This is madness," he said in a huff. He stormed forward, a sudden sense of urgency in his heart.

"We must get off this trail," Bardano said, interrupting what appeared to be a heated debate among Grim-Face, Tarsazi, and Zlata.

Zlata shot him a deadly look. Tarsazi and Grim-Face glanced at each other with concern in their eyes.

"Have you seen something?" Grim-Face asked, his voice muffled by his heavily scarred face.

"Nay, bit it is madness to travel the most obvious path without even the cover of the trees. True the path is narrow, but it widens here and there and twists past many nooks. We are sure to be ambushed!"

Zlata gestured down the rocky path and into the forest, angrily punching her open palm.

"She argues that we will fight one way or the other," Tarsazi said. "This we knew as we set out."

Bardano glanced down into the trees. Mist slithered like ghostly snakes among the boles, and sent a shiver up his back. "I like not the trees, but there we might ambush the ambusher. With luck we might slay a few and break out."

Zlata shook her head and Tarsazi began to argue against Bardano.

"No," Grim-Face cut him off. "I do not trust the forest, but I like the confines of this path less. Though a fight is unavoidable, the enemy's main force will surely block the path. I agree with Bardano."

The argument went back and forth in sharp whispers, Klelia joining in to speak aloud Zlata's thrusts in a too strident feminine voice. The debate was joined by the sound of rocks tumbling down the steep slope to the forest floor below. Zlata gestured vigorously behind them.

"Stop those stupid men!" Klelia shouted, too loud.

The pirates, gathering the direction of the conversation, had left the trail and were scrambling down the incline in a bustle.

Grim-Face made a sound something between a grunt and a laugh. "These are not trained soldiers, lady, that wait about in neat lines 'til commanded. They are pirates.

Zlata's face took on a stoic expression and Klelia muttered a few barbed criticisms, but their case was lost. They followed the others into the trees. Bardano shivered. The air wasn't that much cooler under the boughs, but the mist seemed to penetrate clothing and cling to the skin. His boots made muffled crunches as he marched over the debris on the forest floor. *Has this place changed in a thousand thousand years?* The odd thought simply popped into his head.

"Do you see anything?" He whispered to Eyeboga beside him, as much to see if his voice was muffled as well. It was not.

"No, but it is hard to see far. Does the fog thicken?"

They went on, slow and wary. A bird call cut the air and sent a shiver across Bardano's skin. Without a word, the company came to a halt and dropped low. *An ambush?* He imagined forms skulking just beyond sight. Fearful moments passed as his eyes darted from tree to tree, sweat dappling his brow. The call rang out again.

"There," Eyeboga pointed, and let out a low chuckle. "It is an ugly one."

Bardano followed his gesture. Sitting on a high branch and just visible was a thick-necked, short-beaked bird. He had never seen its like. It seemed content to observe them as they gawked at it. Bardano smiled and let out a quiet 'humph' as they continued. Until the tree it was perched on fell out of sight, the outlandish bird watched them, and the cold tinge of fear touched his guts. His eyes flickered among the branches for long minutes, fearing to see the bird again. *Damn the bird*, he laughed to himself suddenly feeling like a fool. *Eyes on the ground*.

"Look!" Eyeboga choked.

"Let's shoot it this time," Bardano said, thinking Eyeboga had spotted the feathered spy again.

This time, Bardano caught a glimpse of white eyes glowing in a band of black paint. A cannibal. The savage dashed away in a blur of stark black and white limbs.

"Get him before he warns others!" Tarsazi said.

Two of Belgeti's remaining archers let arrows fly, but their target dodged between trees. Zlata shot after him almost as fast as their arrows. The rest of the pirates ran close on her heels. Bardano lost sight of her after a few seconds, and the savage had disappeared into thin air. He eased his sprint as he didn't want to be winded when, and if, he caught the villain. Then he caught a pale flicker of light. Zlata, swords drawn, had crouched low behind a thick thorny bush. She put a finger to her lips and vehemently gestured for him to drop low.

He threw himself down behind a tree just as the pirates swarmed in a few dozen paces behind him. At that moment three score cannibals appeared out of the forest ahead. Bardano gasped at the sight. It was as if they leapt out of tree, earth, and mist – such was their woodcraft. A glance at Zlata revealed her eyes were as wide as his.

With no more need for stealth, a deafening war cry from both sides shook the forest. Pirates and cannibals flew at each other. The savages flew past Bardano and Zlata. As the last of the savages passed him the two groups clashed. He marked one savage at the edge of the fray – for if he attacked their center they could overwhelm him. Bardano surged forward, his limbs quivering in an admixture of fear, rage, and excitement. His sword flashed and he ran one through the back before leaving a red slash on another. He sprang back as four primitive, but deadly sharp, spear tips were thrust at him.

In a series of desperate dodges and parries, he was amazed to find a pirate at his back and his heart still pumping. Brutality followed. Screams of agony and triumph pierced the heavy air. Bardano slashed and stabbed and gasped for breath. Taking a moment to recover, he saw many on both sides were dead, but the savages had the worst of it by far. Grim-Face and Tarsazi fought together as tacticians. Klelia's face was a mask of horror, though she managed to work her sword ably. Zlata, on the other hand was a vision. She was a battle-maiden who danced death. Her swords whirled and flashed out like a serpent's tongue. Spears slipped past her lithe body only to drop to the earth beside their newly slain wielders.

A dozen cannibals fled in a wild rout back the way they had come. With the battle won, a raucous cheer went up. A few pirates lay in the muck and gore at their feet, but far fewer than the enemy.

"At them!" Grim-Face yelled.

Bardano cheered and sped after the fleeing savages, a bloodlust driving him on. Never had he felt a hate that cut so close to the bone. An arrow lodged in the spine of the closest enemy, and he collapsed to the ground. The others sped on and they turned a thickly tree'd hill.

Bardano was among those at the forefront when they rounded the rise. There at last the earth sloped downward, and not far off was the wide mouth of the eastern exit from the Vodionatar. Among the light smattering of trees, not a quarter of a mile from where he stood, swarmed a host of savages.

Grim-Face grabbed Bardano as if he might charge at them. "There must be a few hundred of them!"

"Aye, and they've seen us!" Bardano said.

A roar like a wave passed over the long column of cannibals guarding the eastern pass. They pounded their spears on the ground, gathered into a semblance of a military line, and marched toward them.

"Move back!" Grim-Face said.

None balked at his command and Bardano turned back up the slope into the Vodionatar with the rest of them.

"Where do we go? Back to the castle?" he asked Grim-Face as they rounded the hill again.

"Back to that prison? My heart tells me that way is blocked. Perhaps we fight."

Zlata signed and gestured as best she could, as Grim-Face and Tarsazi devised a desperate plan. Then Eyeboga, who had held back to watch the advance of the savages, came sprinting forward and calling out. They awaited him by a tall, pointed outcropping of stone.

"They have stopped," he said breathlessly.

"What's that?" Grim-Face said. His voice expressed an incredulity that his scarred face could not.

"The brutes rushed halfway up the hill, and have stopped. They but block the path."

Grim-Face shared a dire look with Tarsazi. "They keep us trapped in this strange place. That grizzled bastard of a shaman is brewing something. Skarde was right."

"The *Baronetta* was right. She warned you all." Klelia said.

"We'd all be stuck in that stone hut of yours still if not for Skarde," Bardano said.

"Quiet!" Grim-Face shouted.

Zlata made a sharp gesture for silence at the same time.

"Let's fight," Bardano said refusing Grim-Face's command. "A sudden and well-organized attack..."

"No," Grim-Face said. "They outnumber us twenty to one. Let us return to the high stone path. At least there our archers can expend their arrows before we die."

All the company wore gloomy masks upon their faces, but no one made an objection. They trudged back the way they came, and with every step the fog seemed to thicken. Bardano followed keen-eyed Eyeboga, but soon even he took pause to get his bearings. The southern cliff face of the Vodionatar was wholly obscured, and the black shafts of the trees held a waiting menace. The meager trail diminished, and they found themselves in a thick copse of trees.

"Where is the path?" Bardano said. "This fog is unnatural."

They wandered forward, guessing the right direction. Bardano's hair stood on end as they went on, picking their way through thick brush. They found a path, but soon it led to a tall, pointed outcropping of stone. He stared at it in horror. They had but circled back upon themselves.

Then, far off, they heard a keening sound – a human voice raised in a death throe, the last tortured breath of a soul consigned to hell. The men froze, and Bardano listened like one spellbound.

"Have you lost a whistle?" Bardano said to Zlata. "Could it be one of the damnable things."

Zlata shook her head.

"Aye," Tarsazi said. "That is the voice of a mortal man."

"It's making me dizzy, whatever it be," Savo said.

"Aye," Bardano said. "It fills my head. It's like hands are gripping my skull and are trying to pull it apart!"

"A spell, it is," Eyeboga said to Bardano. "Keep your wits about you!"

Bardano ran toward the sound, or where he thought it came from. "Is it moving? It seems to be all around us!"

The trees seemed to move. *A trick of the light?* One of the men yelled in confusion and pain, followed by another. Bardano gripped a tree trunk with his left hand and turned to look at his fellows. They were all yelling now, or growling, or screeching. Some doubled over, and their limbs slowly twisted into feral shapes. Some grew claws, and others' eyes blazed huge and inhuman. Others seemed to rot, or they took on snake-like features.

Bardano's heart froze in supernatural terror. By a trembling act of will, he released his iron grip on the tree and backed away from the mad scene. Some were already dashing into the fog obscured woods. There was an almighty clash and two of the monstrous figures bashed at each other, locked in a mortal struggle. Bardano watched spellbound as they tore at each other, until one finally fell. The victor... what mad mix of beast and nightmare was it? The victor turned on him and charged.

"Luwydi's curse!" Bardano spat, and he fled as quickly as his legs would carry him.

Belgeti struggled against tight rope at his wrists. His dry mouth burned. He struggled to lift his head. His eyes, too, burned, and when he tried to open them his head swam. He coughed in a dry wheeze, and spent a long minute just trying to catch his breath.

"The old horsey stirs," he heard Hochnay mutter over a commotion.

"Have respect carrot-head," Belgeti hissed dryly. "I have twenty summers on you."

He wasn't sure that Hochnay had heard him. A woeful racket of chanting and whooping, drums pounding, and the shuffle of capering feet came from all around him. Again, he forced his eyes open, and though his vision blurred he saw enough to set his heart quivering.

A hundred or more cannibals danced in ecstatic frenzy before a fearsome megalith. It was a stone shaped like a distended skull, fifteen feet in height, and its toothy gaping maw seemed to tug at the very breath in Belgeti's lungs. He knew, as one knows in a dream, that it was old beyond old, and millennia had patted across its dome like raindrops.

Kampu stood before its jaws, his arms raised, chanting in a rapturous timbre rising to madness. He shook his staff and turned to direct the blasphemous riot of his devotees. Belgeti tugged at his binds. They held fast. He was tied with rough rope to a stake driven deep into the ground.

"It seems we've come to our end," Belgeti said with a laugh, but his mirth was defiance, and his voice cracked.

"Aye," Hochnay said, his voice rougher than usual. "If only I could get free, I'd rammy mah way to the afterlife."

Belgeti shut his eyes and prayed silently to his gods for a chance, at least, to die in combat and not be butchered and eaten like a pig. His thoughts wandered though, and he saw the faces of his sons and daughters. How he wished to ride tall in the saddle beside them again.

"Keep your eyes open," Vajda said, her voice like silver bells dragged over pebbles. "I have a blade in my vambrace. If only I can work it into my palm..."

Belgeti looked down the line of captives. Past Vajda, Ramzi and Oğuz were fixed to stakes, still swooning from the mephetic smoke. Skarde was no where in sight.

"Have they slain the Captain?" Belgeti said.

"I've nay seen him since those howlin' bastards smoked us. He may have gotten away," Hochnay said.

That, at least, cheered Belgeti. He found the strength to look about. The otherworldly Great Skull Totem was the black heart of a henge of grey-black slabs to which scrubs and lichen of an alien look grew. The staggered monoliths rose toward the pallid sky like the decayed bones of titans turned to stone. He felt a sudden chill. Here, the air itself seemed out of place and time. This place had remained unchanged and untouched for many ages of the world, as the mountain had risen about it on either side, or so he imagined. A primeval curse lay between the unnatural cliff faces, and here was the source. An antediluvian sorcery made for some purpose he knew not, and inimical to mortal men.

With those dark thoughts filling Belgeti's head he watched the old shaman twirl and leap like someone possessed. He pounded his staff on the ground and turned to the captives. With a maniacal expression on his face he screamed a command and levelled a clawed hand at Oğuz. A few savages surged forward. They cut his bonds with a flint blade and lifted the semi-conscious man up.

"Ye painted cowards!" Hochnay yelled, followed by a lavish assortment of insults in the Commorian tongue.

"It's no use," Vajda said. "I have my blade half-way out."

"Save a few for us," Belgeti said, though he could not muster even a half-hearted laugh.

He watched helplessly as the brutes shred and tore Oğuz's clothes away. They lifted his naked body and tossed him into the gaping mouth of the Skull Totem. They held him in place, though he did not struggle. Was it a blessing that he was not fully conscious? *No*, Belgeti thought, *none of this is a blessing.*

Now Kampu spat out an unholy sermon, and the savages were whipped to new heights of passion and frenetic dance. Suddenly, Oğuz struggled. He lifted his head and stared in wide eyed terror at the monstrous shaman and the unholy chaos about him.

"No! Get away!" he screamed.

He fought against their grip, but they held on with ecstatic strength. The Og-Riz raised a black obsidian knife and chanted an obscene spell. His voice rose over the others, and stirred a primal terror deep in Belgeti's mind. The others also watched, rapt in horror. Like a striking cobra, Kampu's knife dove at the man's bare flesh. The black blade pierced low in his gut, and he screamed and ear-piercing scream as if all the souls in Hell wailed through his open mouth. Kampu dragged his blade up Oğuz's body, splitting him like a ripe fruit. Blood and viscera tumbled out even as the demonic shaman cut through his sternum right to his clavicle. Belgeti, who had seen death, both frequent and gruesome in war, quailed and turned away from the unholy scene.

The sky darkened, or perhaps it was Belgeti's eyes that dimmed. But the Great Skull Totem came into awful clarity. Kampu took a bowl and dipped it into his victims open belly. He held the red dripping vessel above him and drank a bloody draught.

He thrust his claw-like hand into his victim's chest and withdrew Oğuz's heart, which glistened in the unnatural light. He tossed it into the maw of the totem. The weather worn eyes of the skull glowed with unsavory light. Kampu turned to the wild mob, his white beard drenched in gore, and his eyes flickered like the skull's did.

The fog about them thickened. The four assistants of the grisly ritual pushed Oğuz's broken remains further into the skull's maw, and it disappeared. Belgeti blinked. His eyes were still red and pained from the smoke. Had the skull swallowed the body? He saw monstrous and evil forms lurking in the corner of his eyes. When he glanced at them, they were but the capering forms of the painted cannibals – menacing, but still men. He imagined howls and demonic cries in the air. He saw, more with his minds eye than eyes of flesh, the Skull Totem belch up wispy figures: fog-zephyrs which slithered away on evil errands.

He shut his eyes and prayed to his gods again to blot out the horror. How long did the madness go on? The savages came and took Ramzi, and he, Hochnay, and Vajda could only look on in horror as the ritual was repeated. When the unbearable sacrifice was over and the skull again seemed to swallow the corpse, Vajda looked at them with wide eyes on the verge of frenzy.

"I have my knife! I... I can free us in a moment!"

"Do it quick, I beg you," Belgeti said. "I wish to die on a spear tip."

"Aye," Hochnay said hoarsely.

Terrible minutes dragged on as Belgeti and Hochnay watched as she struggled to cut the bonds with no more leverage than she could provide with her fingers. She gave them a scowl but once, for otherwise she kept her blue eyes on the dancing cannibals. Too late, she was, as Kampu barked a command and pointed to Vajda. Her face wrinkled like a snarling animal, and she redoubled her efforts, but Belgeti knew it was in vain.

Before they reached her, a thunder-crack of a battle cry went up. Belgeti's heart froze. Was this a new force of cannibals or had some army appeared from out of the hopeless mists? Belgeti's eyes darted about. Then he caught sight of the intruder, and a hundred pairs of eyes were turned the same way. Upon a great rock just outside the circle of megaliths stood a mighty lone figure, sword held high.

Skarde had returned.

Chapter Thirteen

Still choking from the foul fumes, Skarde staggered onward. His head still spun as if he were intoxicated. How he escaped, he knew not, but blood dribbled from his sword. He took a moment to rest and ponder his situation. He guessed he went south, but in the confusion, fog, and thick forest he knew he might be wrong. *Move*, he thought, *stay a straight path. I will come to the foothills, the east way, or one of the rock faces sooner or later.*

Scanning the trees and wary of the enemy, he crept forward. The south cliff face revealed itself through the boughs and Skarde sighed in relief. It occurred to him that, with his woodcraft, he might pass unseen like a ghost, east or west, and find a road to wherever the whims of his heart might take him. *No,* he thought, *I am still the Captain, and I can not abandon Belgeti, Hochnay and the rest to be cannibal fodder. Not even those cursed women.*

An inhuman shriek chilled his skin. Frozen for a moment in supernatural terror, he forced himself to turn. With a wooden shamble he stumbled in the direction from which it had come. A thick fog appeared as if from the ground. Deep in the mists, hidden from his eyes were growls, and bestial shouts, and the occasional ring of steel. He squatted low, hidden in a patch of bushes, and listened for a tense minute. No threats were near him. *What happened?* He tried to piece the chain of events together, but nothing quite made sense.

He stalked. Moving, crouching, listening. He kept to the brush, passing stony patches, trees, slopes, and dips. Though he moved with vigilance, he became impatient for a change in the terrain. He knew he had missed something, and it seemed that hours had passed. Confusion and fear scratched away at his consciousness. Did some of the trees leer at him with loathsome faces?

Then he came to the edge of a long dark patch of grassy field, and beyond that, there seemed a warm glow. Was this the eastern exit? He heard yet another howl in the distance. Any change in this cursed place was welcome. His sharp eyes peeled away the layers of mists to either side and before him. Seeing no threats, he ran forward. The light seemed to come no closer.

"Nine Hells," he cursed.

He knelt and touched the clump of grass that poked up from mats of leaves, and the scent of wet trees, moss, and earth filled the air. *It's real,* he thought. *This is no dream.* Glancing up, he saw the dark trunks of trees behind him. *How? I left them behind.* His musing was cut short as the thud of heavy footsteps and a deep, brutish snarl. Skarde bounded up and held his sword before him as an eight-foot tall grey-black monster charged him.

Huge, clawed hands swiped at him, and Skarde jumped out of the way with the speed of a great cat. Its hunched slimy body spun to face him, and snarled again with its distended, fang filled jaws.

"A troll!" Skarde gasped.

He leapt back, shocked to come face to face with this creature of legend, swinging his sword defensively.

Reach out to me!

Skarde, his mind reeling, pushed the voice of the evil sword away. Then, in sudden rage, he slashed doggedly and pressed forward.

"Back, demon!"

The troll knocked his sword aside and bellowed in rage, yet Skarde almost heard words in its animal howling. He sprang back again. Was the mystery of this enigmatic place a clan of Trolls? Did they guard some monstrous relic of legend? The thought flit into his head, and as quick, he set it aside as the creature sprang forward. Skarde felt a quiver of zeal from his sword. He slashed with all his might, and the troll's claw fell from its maimed arm. Quick as a snake he spun the blade and plunged it into the troll's guts.

It wailed in agony and dropped to the ground.

Skarde turned and ran. *Too easy*, he thought. He imagined trolls to be as he had just seen, but stories held them to be dealers of death; creatures that could ruin a whole village of warriors. He shook his head. Where was the light? Gone.

"This is madness!" he yelled.

Whispers in the mist seemed to mock him. What words they said were unclear, but they were words of fear and despair, that much he felt. *Do monsters await me at every turn?* Now he heard hateful laughter among the trees.

"No!" Skarde bellowed. "You lie to my ears. You lie to my eyes."

He closed his eyes and shut out the madness around him. *A spell*, Skarde thought. *That shaman – may the Gods damn him. Now he weaves his loathsome magic. If I am deceived, I will be in chains.* Skarde squeezed the hilt of his sword until his wrist burned with the strain. *That is real. The sword is real. The smell of the dew on the grass is real.*

Then Skarde heard a yell from afar. The voice was angry, fearful, but human. He focused on that and pushed the whispers and wails in the air aside. Opening his eyes, he gazed at his fist gripping his sword. His eyes ran along its blade, and finally out beyond. There, the mists had parted. Heavy clouds lay overhead, and in the distance, the stone cliffs of the mountain lay behind the line of treetops beyond. He breathed deep, looking about for threats. Here was reality.

He had overcome the power of the *weird*.

Another soul wrenching scream echoed through the woods. "Curses of P'thon!" he swore, and he turned his feet in that direction.

His injured leg burned, and his heart pounded as he made his way by instinct. He wondered what he might find, now that the *weird* was lifted from his mind, and what he could do to stop it. *Kill Kampu, I suppose*, in answer to his second question. The answer to his first question appeared as a grizzly vision on the ground before him.

"Farasid..." Skarde could barely whisper in a tremulous voice.

His companion since their escape from the wizard's isle lay curled in a pool of bloody viscera, his sword blade laying near but broken in two. Skarde came to a dead stop, drawing no breath as icy fingers wrapped around his stomach.

Gutted, and his 'Claw' broken... I did this. Skarde's jaw clenched in rage. He now bitterly wished the illusion still had hold of his senses to spare him the sight. *Now you join your brother in the halls of the fallen warriors. Speed you well.*

For a long moment, he stood stunned, until a keening wail sounded faint but cruel in the distance.

Fool, make haste! My men are killing themselves. He swiveled his head to-and-fro and seeing no one near, he ran. He did not know where to go, but by some instinct he chose to seek the center of the cleft between the mountains. He kept his eyes keen for any sign of movement and stopped again and again to listen for his allies, now enemies by dint of madness.

Something flew overhead, a shrieking terror, heard now more in his mind like the voice of the spirit in his sword. And likewise in the vision of his mind, he saw a phantasmal creature carrying in its talons, like a gigantic bird of prey, a ghostly human figure. There, yet not there, it was hard to track, but he turned his steps as best he could in that direction.

A sudden feeling of urgency gripped him, and he ran. He came to a tumble of giant grey stones. They formed a low hill of blocks. He sped up a path and hopped atop the peak. Before him was a scene of horror. A small army of cannibals capered wildly about a ring of monoliths. Kampu, his face and arms blood drenched, raved like a madman. The twisted shaman snarled a command, and his brutish servants made for his friends, all bound to stakes nearby.

Morsfangsel laughed in its scabbard. Skarde could hear its cruel jesting in his mind. It spoke not to him, and he knew it cared little what path he now took. Gritting his teeth, Skarde stood boldly forth, no longer caring for stealth.

"Thunir!" He thundered, and he thrust it defiantly skyward. "Pray, look upon me, and lend me the strength of body and strength of will for the battle before me! And if I should live, whatever comes after!"

Hundreds of eyes turned to regard the lonesome warrior standing upon the rocks. Some laughed, thinking him still maddened by the spell Kampu even now wove. He leapt from stone to stone down into the ring of monoliths to the ground his foes stood upon. Those nearby ceased laughing, seeing the fire and fury in his eyes.

Now, Morsfangsel, I embrace your power! Let us go forth and slay!

Skarde held his sword high and charged forward, rage boiling. He let his conscious mind slip away as a storm unequalled crashed over him. He raised a battle cry, and it was also the voice of Mor. He sprinted forward faster than a courser stallion, evading the two dozen spears that were hurled toward him. Two or three of the projectiles struck home, but hardly pierced his skin deeper than a finger's width.

He felt pain, but it stung him more like an insult than a wound. A half dozen savages charged him, spears raised. Like a blast of thunder, he swept his sword before him, and the hafts of the weapons splintered like kindling sticks. Their razor-sharp tips had not yet fallen to the ground before he swept his blade back and separated a cannibal's torso clean from his hips. Another he spitted upon his sword and hurled him arcing through the air as if he were as light as a scarecrow.

Screaming in a craze, the weaponless men grappled his limbs, two to each side. Those he flung aside as if they weighed no more than rabbits. The two that grappled his right crashed against a megalith thirty feet away, their bones cracking. Those on his left, he sent like mangonel stones into their fellows, killing them. Frustrated but undaunted, his savage attackers surrounded him. They called to their gods, swore oaths, and refused to give ground to the Northern berserker who was deadly beyond the measure of mortal men.

For Skarde, for Mor, there was nothing in the world but blood and battle-lust.

Skarde hacked limb and flesh and skull. Blood flew skyward and painted the earth. Screams of death and fury filled the air. Skarde's blade was a flickering doom, and his fist fell like a mace. How long did this charnel dream go on? His voice, the voice of Mor also, bellowed for blood and violence. Yet now, between his red curses, he heard an otherworldly cry from beyond the grave. It pressed against his consciousness. Before the Great Skull Totem loomed a giant creature with a horned skull, a hulking reptilian body, and tentacle arms, draped in shadow.

"You are the weapon I shall take in my hand. You, my slave, shall bring death to all defilers of my land."

The few cannibals that still lived became a swarm of mind-blasting alien forms. The mountainous voice spoke, its very words shaping reality.

"No!" Skarde shouted. Or was it Mor?

Skarde took step after step toward the thing which seemed to grow as he approached. Foes with madly grinning faces lashed out at him, but those he cut down with desperate strokes. The remainder fled, wailing in agony and madness.

The chimeral horror before him was the last threat, and Skarde was determined to kill it. That such a thing should even exist in the world sickened him, and he felt like a man drowning.

Madness and black dread overwhelmed him. Did he fall to his knees? Did he now crawl? He found himself before the demonic thing. Mor screamed in defiance as he did, and whether it was by his will, Mor's will, or both combined that dragged him forward, he never knew.

"Kneel and know you are not, and never were, anything, but my servant. You will bring death and feed Him." The wraithlike voice echoed in his skull.

Some last shred of rational thought burst into Skarde's mind – he knew that this *Him* was master the of these evil spirits, and the magic that bent the mind. Not a man but some *thing*, a being whose essence twisted this strange place and brought madness. Kampu, he guessed, dared to bargain with the monstrous miscreation housed since time untold in the Great Skull Totem.

"I bring death," Skarde grunted, and with the very last shred of his will, he leapt up and struck out with his blade.

The grotesque thing screamed, and the world was filled with the wailing of uncountable tormented souls. Skarde fell shuddering to his knees, clutching his ears. His blade clattered to the cold hard stone. The landscape twisted into nightmare forms, and he shut his eyes.

It is a trick! Skarde repeated to himself. *I will not be fooled again!* Gasping for breath, Skarde sought out his sword, and finding it he forced his eyes open. Before him Kampu's head lay separated from his body, yet his eyes fixed on Skarde's.

"I will walk again!" said the ashen head.

Chapter Fourteen

In a moment both dreamlike and uncanny, the heavy fog lifted. Bardano held the hilt of his sword close to his breast and remained silent and unmoving under the great curving arms of a tree that clung to a rocky shelf. His hands shook. Even after he hid from the monsters, shrieks that froze both his body and spirit had cut the air. He strained to listen for long minutes for any hint of those devils. A wearied silence hung over the forest.

Then, like a prowling cat, he drew himself up into a crouch. His eyes darted this way and that. Satisfied that no horrors lurked nearby, he picked his way carefully forward. By the light, he gauged his orientation. *If only I could see the sky uncloaked by these accursed trees*, he thought. He stalked forward, almost certain of his eastward course. He crept on until something rustled the hairs on the back of his neck. He darted into a thicket and listened. A faint rustling of forest detritus set a cold stone in his stomach. Whatever it was, it was near.

Whirling around the trunk, he held his blade ready to slash or parry. Ten paces away stood a man, blade also ready, with a face scarred and slashed to disfigurement.

"Grim-Face!" Bardano's voice crackled. "Is that you or a phantom?"

"Bardano," Grim-Face said warily. "Are you in command of your senses?"

"Aye," Bardano said, "but I have seen monsters and mad visions and this terrible forest seems to twist about like a prison without walls. What happened?"

"I know not. Some evil sorcery is afoot – or was," Grim-Face said. "Has the spell been broken?"

Grim-Face slowly lowered his sword, and Bardano did likewise. The two came together in a rough clinch, slapping each others' backs as much to reaffirm their solidity as their camaraderie.

They went on, and though a thin mist slipped through the forest like chill fingers, it did not befuddle their senses. Far off, they heard someone yelling. Moving quickly but quietly, they caught sight of figures darting between trunks ahead of them. They drew their weapons and prowled forward, watchful of an attack.

"Ho!" Bardano yelled. Certain that they had been seen so that stealth was pointless. "Are you pirate or nay?"

They were met with silence, and over a small outcrop of rock Zlata sprang up holding her swords before her. She gestured at her head, and then at him.

"What do you think, woman?" said Bardano, laughing a little too loudly.

Zlata's eyes narrowed, not at all amused at his answer as Grim-Face was. She slid her swords back into their scabbards and jumped from the outcropping. Unimpressed by their apparent levity, she led them on after pointing to her eyes and ears.

"That ghost-haunted fog may have passed," Bardano said with the airs of a king's counselor. "But we may be swarmed by cannibals at any moment."

Zlata looked darkly at him with crossed brows and went on. After some half hour, they came near to the passage at the eastern end of the Vodionatar. There, half the crew waited and watched with cautious eyes. They met Tarsazi with joy. Comparing stories, they found all had suffered madness.

"Death and horror," Tarsazi said. "Monsters came and went with the mist. There are bodies in the woods. Our men... slain by those foul monsters!"

"Summoned by that damnable bone-caster," Bardano said. "Be this all that is left of us?"

Tarsazi's answer was cut short by shouting. Eyeboga came dashing from a thick copse, his breath ragged.

"The savages..." he managed between panting breaths.

"They come?" Tarsazi threw his hands into the air. "Are the gods so angered with us they show us no respite? We are three dozen, and they number in the hundreds. We can only flee!"

Eyeboga shook his head and waved his hands as he puffed. "They fight..."

"They fight who?" Grim-Face asked with a strained voice.

"Each... other..." Eyeboga said.

Bardano, Tarsazi, Grim-Face, Zlata, and a few others each looked to the other for a sign of understanding. None were to be had.

"Mayhaps we should all go and see for ourselves what the cannibals are up to?"

"Aye," Tarsazi said as he came to grips with his panic. "Agreed. Let us go down as one group. There is little benefit in stealth now."

Eyeboga led them to a ridge high on the hill which they had previously rounded. Bardano imagined that the high rocky path wound somewhere above them. They kept low to the ground as the trees gave way to open sky. They gazed down the hill's steep slopes and on the field below they watched a perplexing battle play out. The cannibals fought each other in a wild melee. In the chaotic brawl Bardano discerned that three roughly equal groups seemed determined to kill each other.

"Why? Is this Skarde's doing?" Bardano said to himself.

"Brothers, behind us!" Eyeboga shouted.

Like an apparition summoned by its naming, a figure appeared. All eyes turned to the marching figure – a huge, nearly naked form holding its sword at its side. Even in the dismal grey light, it stood out red and glistening like an open gash peeling itself out of the mist. Bardano's eyes widened. Skarde had returned, soaked from crown to foot in gore. No one, not even himself dared approach, as it seemed the horror of the weird had returned. On both sides the others gaped in mute dread. Some twenty cautious paces behind the horrific form of their captain came Belgeti, Hochnay, and the Baronetta.

"Skarde?" Bardano said as the blood drenched giant loomed uncomfortably close.

Skarde halted before them and his hard, unfriendly eyes scanned them. "Aye, that is my name," he said after a long pause.

"What happened?" Bardano asked.

Skarde stood silent and wore an unfathomable expression on his face. Belgeti approached them, but walked about Skarde, giving him a wide berth.

"He killed the Shaman," Belgeti said. "And a hundred or more cannibals."

The statement seemed absurd. Yet Bardano accepted it, given Skarde's gruesome appearance and the nightmare-like happenings of the day. Skarde strode forward heedless of those in his path. The men backed away from the blood-stained giant. He stared over the ridge to view the battling tribes of cannibals.

"They fight," Skarde said, his voice stentorian and harsh. "Good. One of the worms who escaped me has brought them word of the death of their spiritual leader. Even now they break into factions, vying for control as I knew they would. Come, we can make our escape now."

"No. Klelia may be lost or captured... and there may be other survivors," Vajda said.

"She's right," Belgeti said.

Skarde looked at him as if betrayed.

"Even if they are all dead, I would not leave their flesh to be desecrated by these cannibals. This place is otherworldly and hateful. We can not leave them here," Belgeti said.

"We go, now!" Skarde said.

"Do I waste your time?" Vajda said. Her hand, resting on her hilt, trembled. "Then begone. I will lead the men and do what is needed if you are unable."

"You dare to defy me? You die!" Skarde bellowed.

He raised his sword. Like a lash she drew her steel and struck. Skarde blocked it but was on the defensive as her sword flashed in arcs. Their blades rang out like chimes, cold and deadly. For a long moment, Skarde did not counterattack. Belgeti caught a stern look in his eyes, his eyebrows wrenched in effort, and his lips drawn tight.

At last, he knocked her sword away, and she almost lost her grip on it. He swung down at her, and she danced skillfully out of the way. For a moment there was a desperate back and forth.

To Belgeti it seemed that Skarde displayed none of the inhuman speed and strength he had at the Skull Totem. Then, he was a living demon, a monster in the image of a man. Now, Skarde seemed to tremble as if fighting against his own limbs.

"No!" Skarde grunted. "No."

The Baronetta, seeing an opening, stabbed at him. He parried the blade, reached out to grab her cuirass, and with one hand tossed her back twenty paces. Skarde dropped his sword, grabbed his head, and fell to his knees. Even as he did so Vajda landed. In her own nigh supernatural display of agility, she landed on her feet. Right away she raced back at him.

She screamed a battle cry and swung her sword in a glistening arc at Skarde's exposed neck. The clash of steel rang out as Belgeti leapt forward and interposed his blade.

"Fool! He is a devil. Kill him before he kills us!" Vajda said.

"Nay... look. He fights a battle unseen!" Belgeti said.

Chapter Fifteen

Skarde could not lower his sword arm. He fought to release his grip and one by one his fingers peeled away. The sword tumbled to the ground. He followed, and he fell to his knees.

The world darkened. Then, a hot flickering light touched Skarde's eyelids. He lifted his head from the cool dirt under his forehead, and gazed upon the giant, Mor, towering above him. Under the black sky, Mor's obsidian skin blazed a glossy red reflecting the flames that issued from his copper hair and beard. Smoke curled from his fingers, clenched into fists and his eyes blazed in diabolic triumph.

Looking up at the godlike apparition, Skarde clenched his teeth. "You! You will not master me."

Mor laughed. "Cast my prison aside, then."

"You will dominate another and seek to slay me."

"What matters that, mortal? Your life is a flickering flame, snuffed out in a moment. What matters a few years."

"You are my servant," Skarde said, straining to stand against some great weight that seemed to lay upon him.

Mor barred his iron-like teeth as Skarde stood and glared at him with defiant eyes. As he stood, the giant seemed to recede into the distance.

"My fire is lit now in the forge of thy soul. Ye will not know peace until thou hast avenged me. Only then shall thy crime against me be forgiven." Mor's voice boomed even as he faded into a swirling cloud of smoke and ash that surrounded them both. He faded from view, but his voice came again as if from afar. "Thou art but a mote, mortal, and I shall ne'er be unhoused again!"

Skarde coughed smoke from his lungs. The world spun and he came face to face with the floor of the forest. Gasping for air, he remained on all fours, exhausted. He felt as if he had been squeezed by a giant hand, and a terrible fatigue lay upon him. At last, he stood... and staggered.

"Hey," Belgeti shouted. "He stirs. Come help me get the brute up."

Feet scuffled the dank detritus of the forest floor, and hands grabbed him. He grunted and shuffled away their grips, and with a lurch, he stood under his own power. For a moment, he stared into the forest where the vision of the giant had been, his sight blurred, and his eyes burning. His limbs felt as if fettered by heavy chains, but he fought to stand steady and upright.

"What happened?" Belgeti said, and several others stared on.

"'Twas my old friend, Mor," Skarde groaned. "Now that I've invited him to share a drink, he thinks he owns the hall."

Belgeti nodded and Skarde gazed about in confusion. He was in a thickly forested dell and a small creek trickled nearby. Two dozen of his men lay on the slopes, resting as they could.

"We had to move, if you even recall coming to the hilltop. You are too damn heavy. A mighty troop of cannibals came fleeing through to get back to the western side of the Vodionatar. Things went poorly with their cousins on the eastern side, I suppose."

"Be this all that is left," Skarde said, scanning the paltry number of men with them.

"Nay," Belgeti said. "Another dozen men along with the Baronetta and Zlata have built litters and gone looking for survivors... or the dead."

"Good," Skarde said. "We can not leave any more to that fate. I will help them." Skarde lifted himself from the ground, and his body ached to the core.

"You had best not, friend. Hochnay is a natural storyteller and wove quite a tale of the slaughter. Vajda also told tales with a more sinister air. The men are spooked after... all that has happened. You should clean yourself up. You look, *and smell*, like a slaughterhouse."

Skarde held up his blood crusted arms and nodded. "I remember it all, Belgeti," he said. "Yet it feels like a dream. Both distant and real."

"Was that really you," Belgeti asked.

"Yes... and no. My head hurts to think on it." Skarde said no more and made his way over to where the little stream burbled enough to scoop up handfuls of water. As he did, he realized his leg hurt no more. He pulled off the bandage, and the wound looked as if it had weeks to heal. He splashed himself with water, too tired to wonder yet even at a miracle. The bracing caress of the cold, clean, water revived his senses, but he began to shiver as he had not in years. The earth pulled on his limbs, and he nearly gave into the temptation to lie down. Behind him the trickling stream had turned red as an omen.

At last, men began returning. Their faces grim, they bore one dead compatriot after another. Skarde watched the intermittent procession, and solemnly acknowledged each one, though he said nothing. Two men carried past him the bloodied corpse of Klelia. Her ghost pale face carried no memory of pain or fear, but of determination. An arrow with black and white striped feathers sprung from her chest.

He knew those arrows to be those used by Belgeti and his archers. So, one of his own had slain her. Any doubts Skarde had about the weirding were gone. *What a terrible power, to twist and depose men's own senses.*

Skarde called together all those who were present, and took counsel. They agreed to build a pyre and wait until dusk. Then they would light it, and travel to the nearest village under the black mantle of night.

Just before the counsel ended, Vajda and Zlata returned over the lip of the dell. A pall of silence fell over the men, and they all fixed their eyes upon her. Her face hardened and Skarde knew that straightaway she felt the doom about to greet her. With solemnity she descended the slope and all parted a way for her.

As she espied Klelia's corpse all color drained from her face. Skarde detected a quaver in her step, but she caught herself, and stood stiff. She gazed long, and without tear, though it seemed she was unaware of anything else in the world. Zlata stood beside her Mistress, her chest huffing, tears rolling silently down her cheeks.

After a respectful moment, the men went dreary about their preparations. Vajda cleaned Klelia's battle-stained face, kneeling long by her side. As the sky darkened, Skarde approached her.

"Klelia deserves better than this," she said. There was now no venom in her voice. Still, Skarde kept a hand on his hilt.

"They all do. They are warriors sworn to fight and die. Let us send them like thunder to the sky. Let us send them to Valhalla."

Vajda rose and sighed heavy. "I know not what power you wield, but it is evil. Such a thing should not be trifled with."

"This I know," Skarde said in a whisper so low, Vajda could barely hear. He stood silent for a moment, pondering what dooms the spirit of Mor held in store him... and his companions.

Rites, brief but somber, were held and the fires were lit. Skarde watched the flames crackle about the bodies, and rise to the uncaring grey-black sky. "Speed you away from this cursed land, and fly to golden halls," Skarde said.

Before the flames could attract unfriendly eyes, they left the Vodionatar. Zlata and Hochnay ran ahead to spy the way, but no savage bedeviled them. Long seemed that night. They trudged on, and the glow of the cloud-hidden moon rose high and then began to sink.

The first rays of the Sun greeted them through a crack in the clouds as they caught their first sight of the village. Ringed by sharpened palisades, the village lay silent, and no busy villagers stirred as would be expected at such a colony. The stout gates hung ajar, wreathed with a hundred ghastly ornaments.

The men halted to gaze despairingly upon it. The Baronetta sped forward and leapt atop a stump of a tree. Skarde gazed at her beautiful face, set with determination, and her blonde hair ringed with the fire of the newly risen sun.

"Listen all who will!" She called out. "There is naught left here. If this, the most defended village has fallen..." She said, pausing for a moment to compose herself. "Tomorrow, Zlata and I will make north and find The Mirvayadroga, the Far Road, which goes through a pass in the savage mountains. I will lead those of good sense who wish to join us. All those who will follow me back to the lands of civilization, follow my sword! The road will be long and hard fought, but none shall stop me!"

She stood like a statue of marble, cold and magnificent, gazing at Skarde as if awaiting his challenge. He held his head high and proud and met her eyes. The men shifted their gaze uneasily between the two and they felt the tension grow sharp as swords.

Then, Skarde nodded in assent, yet held her gaze.

She turned her eyes away at last to address the men. "Search the village for anything you might use on the long road. We rest for a day and leave at the next dawn."

A few men raised their eyebrows at Skarde, not in challenge, but in surprise. Belgeti looked on longest, though he wore a bittersweet look on his face. Skarde kept quiet and for the most part to himself for the day. Night came. At the gates only two watchers were left to guard, changing three times before dawn. Though uneasy and in a hostile land, the men gave in to their exhaustion and slept.

The grey light of the sky hardly penetrated the hut that Belgeti and another archer lodged in. Belgeti stood, silently lifted his pack, his bow, and the quiver with but three arrows he managed to scrounge, then padded out of the hut. He went on light feet to the south end of the village, and there, climbed a ladder up to a thin walkway of woven branches set about the inside of the wall. He peered over the edge, and there, in the dim light, hung a short rope over the edge only a dozen feet away. *So, he has gone. He's not so hard to guess. Even avoided the gate as I thought.* He made his way over to it and turned to hoist himself over the edge. As he turned, he was caught by surprise to see a figure on the ground below, watching him. It was Zlata. His eyebrows flared, and his thumb rubbed the grip of his bow as she climbed the ladder.

"You also wish to go?" Belgeti said. Though beyond the days of his youth, he could still be entranced by a beautiful face, and she was captivating. Still, he held up a hand, ready to pull an arrow even as she approached dangerously close.

"We're alone. If she has sent you to assassinate me, do it now," he said.

Zlata shook her head and stepped closer.

"Why do you come?"

She held her finger to her mouth and looked back warily over the sleepy village.

"Reasons, I gather?" Belgeti said, lowering his voice.

She nodded. She was close enough now that her blade could easily fly out, but it remained sheathed. She came closer still, hopped the sharpened stakes of the wall with the dexterity of an acrobat, and slid down the rope. Belgeti hopped over, with less grace perhaps, but with a strength that belied his age, and he met her on the ground.

Off they ran, southward. Belgeti guessed Skarde would head this way, though the placement of the rope could have been a ruse. He had hoped they could catch up with him quickly before the trail went cold. Belgeti considered himself a man of the plains, a horse-archer. Skarde was a man of tree-choked hills. If he willed, he would not be discovered. Questioning Zlata, he discovered, by a few simple signs and a shrug, was little more suited to woodcraft than he was. Undaunted, they ran on, following a river that meandered down from the mountain and kept a weaving course south. It would be the best route to take to gather food or stop for a drink. As the sun turned downward toward the West and the two despaired of locating Skarde, a prickle of fear crawled up Belgeti's spine.

Appearing as if from nowhere among the trees, a large figure charged them. Wielding a sword, he flew at them and let out a cry of battle. Belgeti and Zlata threw out their swords in answer and froze in a defensive posture.

The hulking form held back an attack and tossed back his blond mane in laughter.

"You bastard," Belgeti spat, and eyed Skarde with a curse in his eyes. "I'm too damn old for games like this."

Zlata held her swords high for a moment longer, and then lowered them as Belgeti giggled like a hyena. Skarde sheathed his sword, grasped his friend roughly about his shoulders and shook him with a laugh. He turned his eyes to Zlata, looking her up and down in a lingering gaze both appreciative and questioning. He motioned them forward. The three kept on until the sun, a pale orb behind thick clouds but sometimes shining through, filtered through the trees to dapple the ground before them.

"How did you know to find me walking south?" Skarde asked.

"When you nodded to Vajda, I knew you did not assent to follow her, but for her to lead the others," Belgeti said.

"Aye, you read me right."

"You do not wish to be captain?"

Skarde's joyful face took on a somber cast. In a rare moment he gathered his thoughts before he spoke. "Did you not witness the slaughter at the Skull Totem? I have killed before, as warriors must. But that was a nightmare vision. I will never forget the blood nor the fevered lust for it. This demon-sword," he said gripping the pommel, "this cursed blade has power over me. I ask you to return to the Baronetta."

"I don't think the Baronetta would care for me as one of her subjects," Belgeti laughed. "Nay, I will walk the road with you. You have a curse, aye, but there is also a star over your head, Skarde. I said I would not return to my clan until I have won a surpassing fame. I would that the sons of my sons will speak of me with their heads held high. In my guts I feel that great deeds to outshine the legends of old await you and your companions, friend. Besides, you'll need a level head with you."

"And you Zlata? I am surprised to see you... though a pleasant vision. Why do you leave the Baronetta?"

Zlata shook her head. She made a shushing sound, finger over her mouth before pointing at the sun and drawing her hand across the sky along its course.

"A tale for later then," Skarde said.

"Where do you go?" Belgeti said.

Skarde looked south and pointed with his chin. "That way."

"And what do you hope to find there?" Belgeti said.

Skarde breathed deep and smiled. "Freedom. I need only my boots to put where I will, and my sword to take whatever I need."

Other Works by Erik Waag

Samuel Rider: Sword and Seventies
Sword and Seventies: Vol. 1 — That Axe Anciently Was Mine
Sword and Seventies: Vol. 2 — Fangs of the Moon Opal
Sword and Seventies: Vol. 3 — Title T.B.A. (Coming Soon!)

Skarde: The Wandering Sword
Citadel of Seven Swords
Weird of the Skull Totem
Blades Against Fear (Short story. Anvil Magazine #2)
Princess of the Shrouded Mountain (Work in progress)

About the Author

Erik lives in a grim and frostbitten kingdom. With a lifetime of passion for fantasy adventure stories he has struck out to forge his own. Besides writing in the little spaces between work, and hanging out with his beloved wife and sprogs, he enjoys heavy metal, playing guitar, medieval history, and weightlifting. He is in it for the sword-swinging thrills.

A Humble Request

You, the reader, the enjoyer of sword swinging tales, matter! You, and the community you are a part of, deserve the most satisfying, most action packed, most FUN stories. Please, let me know @WaagBookson Twitter what you liked, and what you didn't. If you feel I've earned it, please take a moment to RATE and leave a WRITTEN REVIEW (no matter how short) of my work on Amazon, Goodreads, and elsewhere.

Written Reviews, even one liners, are powerful and do much to promote indie authors! I would be most grateful to hear from you.

Thank you!

Erik

Printed in Great Britain
by Amazon